Alana was convinced there was some meaning hidden in the numbers.

If Witi's father wanted to remember a date he would've written it in a calendar. And if it was a birthday then he only had Witi's and Mum's to remember. So why were the numbers tucked inside something that was so important to him? Alana's fascination persisted. Witi started playing along to humour her, but soon even he was starting to think:

What would he want kept secret?

Even from Mum.

What did he want remembered?

That no one else could remind him about.

See? Alana said. Your dad was way too interesting for this to be nothing.

Witi wanted to show his mum. But he didn't. She had enough to worry about these days and unless these numbers magically brought his dad back, they probably wouldn't spark her day.

He thought about the cops, specifically the detective who'd done his best to find his father.

NOR'
EAST
SWELL

For my parents who have always been there
- Aaron Topp

First published by OneTree House Ltd, New Zealand

Text © Aaron Topp, 2022

978 1 99003 501 2

Cover photograph: Photo CPL www.photocpl.co.nz

Printed: YourBooks, New Zealand

10 9 8 7 6 5 4 3 2   2 3 4 5 6/2

AARON TOPP

NOR' EAST SWELL

OneTree
HOUSE

PART I

DUMBASS BLOND NEWBIE

Tomorrow it would be eight years. Eight years of learning to package the feelings and accept the unknown.

When he was a kid, Witi couldn't understand any of it – he just wanted things normal again – but as a teen he felt he was starting to make progress and things were finally getting better.

Yeah, just a little better than the day before.

And the day before that.

Like a new tide covering a shipwreck that tiny bit more. One grain of sand at a time.

Witi wrote that down in his book. He put it on the grass beside him and cradled his guitar on his crossed legs. His fingers picked at the strings as he stared down the courtyard of his college, past the students on their lunch break. How much longer would she be? She'd probably found others more normal to be with, leaving him hanging here on the sliver of lawn between the science and toilet blocks.

The loner whose old man disappeared eight years ago.

Yeah nah, just another thought to package there, eh.

Witi closed his eyes and let the notion drift away with the next few chords. When he opened them again a rugby ball was sitting beside his bare feet. In the distance some of the first-fifteen players had their hands up, prompting him to kick it back. Like it was a natural thing to do. Witi put the guitar down and stood. Which end was meant to be kicked? He'd never bothered to learn that sort of stuff. Team sports seemed like way too much co-ordination. And too much talking to others. In the end he just threw a foot into it. The ball sliced off to the side and onto the roof of the science block.

The students made their way towards Witi. Like a set of six dumpers from the ocean's horizon. Except this wasn't the beach. This was all concrete and vertical walls and big egos with their friggin' ball stuck on a roof. Man, if only these guys were waves. He could handle them. Piece of piss.

What the fuck, said the guy in the middle. Go get our ball.

Witi looked up towards the roof and let out a quiet whistle. Gonna need the caretaker for that.

Just climb up yourself.

Witi looked at the bare wall of the building. Yeah nah, sorry, fullas.

Then throw his guitar up there, Jimmy, said one of the others.

Yeah, do it. That'd be a crack-up, said another.

Witi stood in front of the instrument. He'd stand his ground. Silent-as, but willing to fight with every dirty tactic necessary so not one of them could touch his dad's guitar.

But he wasn't expecting one of them to grab his notebook instead. The lankiest, seven foot of muscle sinew and not much else. His long fingers started swiping pages loudly. He stopped at one point and chuckled.

Alana? Aren't you meant to be gay or something?

The others laughed.

Witi knew how this would play out. No teachers around; guys juiced up on testosterone and what else; no rugby practice today. An injustice of sorts. A mismatch in the food chain. It was all kind of a cliché around here.

Except...

Witi threw the first punch. The other guy might've been tall, but he wasn't expecting it and when it connected comfortably with his chin he tumbled like a falling pine, dropping the book in the process. But it wouldn't stop there – not at this college.

Fists like a swarm of bees.

Stinging from every direction.

Witi dropped to his elbows and knees to cower over the guitar, to protect it. He reached out and snatched his notebook in under his torso. They weren't getting that, either.

He felt more punches, shoves. A foot or two.

Just another hold-down: Hold my breath. Wait for the set to pass. Just keep holding my breath.

The ground vibrated, like a tremor. Something around them was under pressure, frantic even; and with each hit he received he could feel it wanting to break free.

Surprised tones. Aggravated voices. A body landing on the grass next to him. The relief of no more hits. The principal's son, Jimmy, was sitting there, dabbing the flow of blood from his nose with the back of his wrist. There was a new fight carrying on, but by now there were teachers trying to pull bodies apart, making it hard to see who had thrown themselves – and their reputation – into the lynch mob to help him out.

Everyone parted. One guy was left sitting on the grass.

Witi had never seen him before. He was missing shirt buttons and his hair stuck out all over the place. He flicked his head back and with a pass of his palms the strands of blond settled neatly back into place. He wiped blood from his lip and then looked at Witi.

Witi grinned back and even held the stare while the boy was hauled away, flanked by two teachers.

Has everyone round here got a ticket to themselves? Witi heard him ask one of the teachers.

Buggered if Witi knew what he was talking about.

One thing was legit, though – blond boys were a rarity round here. Specially ones not looking for the welcome mat. Dumbass should've known better than to interfere. Dumbass blond newbie.

Witi cradled his guitar and prepared to stand. A teacher offered a hand.

Another group of students started yelling as they piled out of the toilet block next door. There were shrieks and swearing from soaked kids who leapt into the yard to avoid water surging through the door.

Someone shouted, Water's shooting out of the taps and toilets. Someone better get a plumber 'cos I ain't cleaning it up!

OUTTA MY LEAGUE

After school, Witi sat in his Telstar and stared at a fantail on the tip of the bonnet. It stared back at him and for a long time neither budged. Eventually Witi pulled the book from his satchel, opened it and wrote:

Angels and feathers
And wings that soar
Heavy hearts
Anchored to the floor

He slid the book back in the bag. When he looked up again the bird had vanished. Had it just been another delusion? Probably. He hadn't been back to that stuffy doctor's office for a couple of years now. Things seemed to be getting sorted, no dramas, but recently he'd had these visions, growing from something he experienced, first once a month or so, then every other week, then almost daily. Would his mum even have the clinic's details still? Man, he hoped not. Nothing was worth heading back to that building for.

A couple of seniors the same year as him walked past his window. They stared in at him, so he jerked his head back and raised his eyebrows. One turned and said something to the other and they both laughed.

Witi felt the surge inside him:

A fresh short emotional swell, like a wind swell, yeah, nah.

Manageable, just.

A bit of chop, a few whitecaps.

Still, it would be bloody good timing if she …

The passenger door opened and Alana was with him.

Whaddya waiting for? Let's go.

Bout time, babe.

Stop calling me that.

She pulled her hair tie out and wavy brown settled across her shoulders, the surfboard nudging at her head.

C'mon, she said, fixing her seatbelt. The tide turned an hour ago.

He smiled. His ocean now glassy.

They headed east, winding through the blocks of tradies' businesses where most of the college students' parents worked. Every street revealed another new *For Sale* or *For Lease* sign in front of an empty shell of a building. Witi and Alana counted the impact it was having by the empty desks in the classrooms. Students suddenly gone one day, packed up with the parents and starting afresh in some other town.

In the next suburb, each garden with its trees took the space of five from their own neighbourhood. Witi envied the security of the people living in these flash houses.

Jimmy had his nose broken today, Alana said. By some new guy, an Aussie.

I know. Had a ringside seat to it.

Heard you were amongst it. One day you're gonna —

I had them.

I also heard he saved you a few extra bruises. Lucky you'll still be able to surf this arvo.

I had them. Just rolling out my strategy is all.

Pfft, whatever. Good job about Jimmy, anyway.

Yeah, good job, he murmured.

What about when everything exploded in the bathroom, she said. How weird was that?

Much of the rest of the trip was, as usual, in silence. Witi liked the fact Alana didn't feel the need to fill the empty spaces with her voice, like so many of the other girls he knew. The only noise coming from her seat was the whistle from her partially open window whenever he went over fifty-five.

His mum worked in walking distance to home and he couldn't remember the last time she ventured far enough to warrant the use of a car. His dad had bought this one for her with cash he'd saved from the handouts the record company fed him. It'd been brand spanking, straight from the showroom. She told Witi it had been the flashiest set of wheels in the neighbourhood. Everyone thought they were crazy sticking roof racks on it. They didn't under-stand — surfers were a rare breed back then. Those same racks were now forever rusted to the roof, and while sticking the boards on top would give them more room in the car, at a college like theirs, the boards would be gone by the end of first period. Not that it mattered – it was only ever the two them anyway, a couple of water babies bound by solar energy and surfing heritage. Surfers were still rare in this part of the city – an oval ball beat a couple of surfboards every time. Whatever, it wasn't like Witi was complaining.

Not that he thought Alana was a beauty queen or anything, but truth was, she was still out of his league.

You're my only friend, he'd joke to her. But he figured she knew he meant it.

His girlfriend, but not his girlfriend. He didn't think, anyway.

She understood him better than most. Her old man was a waxhead too, eh.

Alana's dad didn't surf anymore, but he did a good job of planting the stoke in her way before he let the spiders and dust take over his boards.

It was their friendship glue, Witi was convinced. She understood when Witi told her: Last night I peeled back the duvet and it formed a barrelling right hander.

He saw weird stuff sometimes, like birds on bonnets, but she never judged him or got freaked out.

And at night he could hear the ocean talking to him over the noise of the traffic and the train track, because he had ocean trapped in his ear again.

The other girls at college didn't get him. Didn't want to. But she did.

And that was sweet with him.

At the end of a gravel road and the start of a tree plantation, the kind where the owners had buggered off for years to let the trees do their thing, Witi turned the engine off.

Look at that, Alana said. He's cute.

She was pointing at the fantail darting in the air at the front of the vehicle.

Man, that's weird, Witi said.

Weird? Bet he reckons you're the weird one.

It then flew over and perched on the farm gate that marked the next stage of their journey, before heading into the shadow of trees on the other side.

Witi swung a bag of wetties and towels over his shoulder and they grabbed a board each. Hanging off the locked gate was a sign number-eight wired to the fence: *Pirate Propaty, No Axecess*. With spelling like that, what was the worst that could happen? They ignored it – like always – and climbed over.

Further down the track, salt began to resonate with the smell of pine. The sound of wind through branches was joined by the beat of the ocean. Holding his head at an angle, Witi could swear it was faint voices calling to him.

They scaled down a small bank, across the boundary fence and out along a bluff overhanging the South Pacific.

Alana went straight to the edge to check on the surf. The swell hadn't dropped since they were here yesterday. She hooted so loud gulls nesting in the cliff took flight, signalling with their screeches the surfers' arrival.

Below them, a decent fall away, a head-high set of waves entered the cove. From up here they could see giant submerged rocks amongst the moving kelp. Every time a wave peaked and peeled off in a left-hand wall, the boulders rumbled together. By low tide these same rocks would be exposed.

No wonder Alana had been in a hurry.

She was already back by the fenceline, halfway changed. She pulled her wetsuit up her legs, hopping on the spot to lift the tight neoprene over her backside. She zipped up her suit and Witi saw the curves a college uniform covered so well. She jogged past and gave him an exaggerated stare, which he returned with a wolf whistle. She stopped at the edge of the bluff and peered over.

She waited.

Waited.

Readied.

She threw her board as far off the ledge as she could.

First wave's mine, slow coach, she yelled and leapt off the headland.

Witi ran to the ledge. Below she was swimming to her board. Once she reached it, she looked up and gestured him to hurry up.

He waved back and finished zipping up his own wetsuit.

Who throws themselves off shit like this these days? Alana does, that's who, and all the bubble wrap in the world couldn't stick to her.

She was the toughest girl he knew, besides his mum.

Alana was into it for the simple raw adventure. Witi got that feeling too, understood it completely, but there was another reason for his deeper affinity with the ocean. His mum once told him that when he was born, the old man took him to the beach and dipped him in an ocean wave, he guessed like some sort of DIY baptism. But ever since his dad vanished, Witi convinced himself that the final dying seconds of energy from that initial wave – something that started much bigger and more powerful and many years before – had found a new life inside him, like some kind of reincarnation had taken place. Even now, eight years since the detective in charge told them they'd stopped looking and classed it as abandonment, Witi still fully believed this.

Hadn't told Alana any of that yet, though.

Didn't want to make out he was competing with her for the ocean's affection, eh, Witi figured. It's not what he meant and she could get huffy. Not keen on kicking around by himself if she bailed on him.

Witi's board spiralled through open space and after lining up the dark green of deep water, he launched after it.

He turned the surfboard back towards the beach and stroked into the first wave of a new set. The surge scooped under and pushed him forward like a giant's silent hand. He floated to his feet and accelerated down the slope. The wave pitched its lip over him. Like so many times before. The fingers on his inside hand clawed into the wave, but where the roar of water would normally be, he instead heard whispers, hundreds of them. Like a concert crowd in a library. Must've lasted only a couple of seconds – the length of the barrel, not long enough for Witi to be convinced. Maybe it was just the angle of the swell. Or the cross-shore wind. Or simply another hallucination to rack up.

Through the daylight ahead he saw Alana sit up on her board, hold an imaginary camera to her eye and click before her own image disappeared up and over the wave. Witi adapted to the wave's mood and carved the surfboard back into the chaos. He found enough energy to push through turns and send feathers of water skyward. The whole ride may've only lasted a few seconds, but by the time he hit the final section and sent his board into the air, the barrel episode with the voices had become irrelevant.

The paddle back gave him an opportunity to watch Alana's ride: she did a series of cutbacks and driving bottom turns in her own way. Witi raised a hand and hooted loudly as she sped past close enough for him to touch her. Witi often thought of surfing as more a wahine than a guy thing anyway. Something to do with wanting to nurture rather than destroy. Same reason it was *Mother* Nature not *Old Man* Nature. Alana was all over this. She attacked waves for sure – last year she made some of the local upstarts feel a little inadequate in the nuts area when they watched her drop in on an eight-foot beast – but she always made it look like she was in no danger, like she'd signed a deal with Tangaroa himself.

Or perhaps it was because she was baptised by a waxhead of a dad too, fully charging on a lifelong connection with the ocean.

You always had the body of a surfer, pal.

I'd often say to your mother, look at his hands, like scoops hanging off tentacles for arms. Yeah, you were a skinny kid too, with feet like paddles. And she'd stick up for you and try to remind me her baby was happy on land. Safe on land. Comfortable amongst the concrete and communities and her reach. But you can't change destiny, son. You were born a surfer.

In the first two years of your life you held my neck and I'd wade into the surf and you'd shriek with glee as each wave smothered us. To you it was fun but the ocean and I were introducing you to something else. That's how your relationship started, up close like a hongi.

When you were three I'd take you out in the waves on small days on my longboard and you'd hold onto my back while I stood and together we rode to land. You didn't know it, but a part of you saw what the petrel sees as it glides across the ocean's surface and you subconsciously learnt about flow and placement.

When you were four you could hold your breath in the bath for over a minute.

Your mum insisted on swimming lessons and you were put up two classes in the first week.

We'd sit up on the dunes by ourselves and watch the other surfers and you'd know the difference between a reo, a roundhouse, and a snap. You said the barrel was king and floaters were overrated. At kindergarten you would walk around with hands like scoops and feet like paddles and tell other kids you were Kelly Slater and they thought you wanted to be a girl. You were born a surfer. You were starting to know it.

When you were five I took you for your first surf and you almost drowned. Back on the beach you vomited up the wave that held you down and said, Again.

And again,

And again,

And again we surfed that year.

Out the back I would tread water next to you and during lulls you'd sit up on your surfboard. I taught you how to see a set coming. I'd push you into the wave as you learnt how to use your scoops and kick your paddles efficiently and you soon managed to co-ordinate your limbs and weight into standing. The first time you turned to me after-wards, all smile and teeth, and I was fist pumping my life away. You thought you'd ridden your first wave, but you'd just learnt to dance with nature.

The next year I sat on my own board next to you and taught you how to read the ocean. Lying in the proper place on the surfboard and paddling was second nature now. You could paddle out the back of the breaking waves with ease. Paddle out of trouble. Paddle back into trouble. Sometimes you'd paddle in circles to pass the time. You'd paddle past others to greet the set of the day before they knew it was even coming at them, because you could read the ocean and they couldn't. You had tentacles for arms and scoops for hands and they didn't. It was your destiny and you were starting to believe it.

When you turned seven I told you to listen to the ocean.

Like, *really* listen. You hear them? Yeah, you did.

You didn't know it at the time, but you started to get a reputation as the grommet who had an uncanny knack of being in the right place at the right time. They thought you were fluky, how'd you catch a wave

over there

in there

out there.

Most of them thought you were a cocky grommet, a seven-year-old wave hog. Needs pulling down a peg or three, they'd say. Nothing a bit of grommet-abuse wouldn't fix. A few of the old guys on the longboards could see it, though. I stayed away from others, but on occasion someone would paddle over to ask how a seven-year-old could do what took them fifty years of surfing to do.

Dunno, I'd say. Must be his destiny.

OFFER A RIDE

Back in the city, Witi and Alana drove past a lone figure walking with a bag on his back and a surfboard under his arm with a wetsuit draped across it. He had a bounce in his step that reminded Witi of the guys in suits rushing for their caffeine fix down the Quay way. He turned his attention back to the road.

But Alana stretched her neck and kept looking. That's him, she said.

Who?

The new guy, the Aussie, she said. Turn around.

What for?

Offer him a ride.

Fuck that. No room.

We'll make some, she said. I'll get in the back.

Witi pulled over and started reversing along the gutter line. Alana said his sigh was unnecessary and wound her window down so she could talk.

Heading far? she asked.

Know where Pirie St is? he asked. Up on the hill?

Alana turned to Witi and he nodded: Yeah, kinda.

Your lucky day, she told him and started to open the door.

But Witi heard him block the door. The rear hatch sprang open and the tip of a new surfboard was sliding gently between the front seats. Witi stared up into the rear-view mirror and felt the car lean towards the footpath as the new kid squeezed into the small space in the back. Then he was staring back at Witi. The resonance of a guitar string accidently plucked peaked then faded quickly.

This yours? he asked Alana.

It's his, Alana said.

Know any Barnsey songs?

A couple.

Cool.

You always scrap on your first day? Witi asked.

He shrugged. I'm meant to be quitting. He held a hand out. Name's Jordy, he said.

Alana grabbed at it. I'm Alana. She pointed with her thumb. This is Witi.

Witi turned in his seat and found himself obliged to shake too.

Hey.

It's not every day you get to have a blue with the whole pride, he said. You looked like you needed a hand.

A blue? Alana asked.

Yeah, you know, scrap? Biffo? he said.

Alana looked at Witi. She had an excited look about her. Almost giggly. But Witi didn't see how having an Aussie in their car was suddenly so fuckin' exotic.

Jordy continued: Your guys' footy wonderkid always that tough with his mates around?

I had 'em, Witi said. Didn't need help.

Nah, no stress, Aussies are the best in the world at helping out the underdog. You're welcome, by the way.

You came all this way to prove that point? Alana asked. Ain't much of a claim.

Farkin'oath it is.

What part of Oz you from? Witi asked.

All of it.

Where-bouts, though?

You know the place?

Nah, not really.

Don't worry about it then. It's got warmer water than this place. Having to wear a full steamer here in summer is bullshit.

So what brings you over to our chilly slice of paradise then? Alana asked.

The backseat was silent. Witi guessed Jordy was thinking about the best answer, or maybe whether they were trustworthy enough to share stuff like that.

The old man got headhunted, he finally said. Thought the fresh start in another country would do me good. Pretty much sums it up.

Witi felt a pat on his shoulder.

Damn, I knew you surfed, mate. You had that look in ya eyes when I was getting carted away, same one ya see everywhere back home. You guys hungry? They better serve pies in the ass-end of the world.

IT WAS COMING

That night the guy on TV told Witi and his mum about Cyclone Trudy's devastation of a popular Pacific island. Buildings had been flattened, trees snapped like twigs; there had been severe flooding, and a child was swept away from its mother's outstretched arm. He said experts predicted the storm would move south and grow, which was later confirmed by the graphics of dense circles and a blood-red rain chart building in intensity and dropping slowly down the weather guy's map.

It was coming.

Afterwards in bed Witi dreamt:

He couldn't see land

Sitting on his surfboard

His feet dangling in the dark ocean

His hands gripping the board's rails to stop him toppling

Yeah, amongst the gale force winds

And stinging sea spray

Hurting his eyeballs and filling his eardrums

Amongst the enormous white caps flashing in the moonlight.

Feeling the violent dips of water beneath him heading towards their destination a thousand kilometres away. Joining energy like blobs of mercury and, by the time the first sets hit New Zealand, the trade winds and sea currents would've worked together to sculpt giant lines of clean groundswell, like no one had ever seen before.

But something wasn't right.

Something else was here too.

He could now see lights in the distance. Machines. Scattered along the shore. And could feel a pulse. Dark and sucking life from everything. Paralysing him in the impact zone.

The first of the monster sets rose in front of him, stretching high enough to shadow the moonlight, before folding and exploding on him and the reef.

Witi sat up in his bed and took deep breaths. He settled back and stared through the darkness.

The bedroom door opened slightly and he saw his mum's silhouette in the yellow light.

You okay? she asked.

Yeah.

That dream again?

Same one.

Tomorrow's —

Just another year, he said.

It'll be eight.

I know. We'll be fine.

I love you, son.

Sure.

She closed the door but the shadow from her feet hung around beneath it.

Your mother always said I must've come from the ocean, pal, and I reckon she was right.

I didn't know my parents and I don't reckon I was born like you and her. Father O at the orphanage down at the harbour said God must've left me on the outgoing tide because I appeared on their doorstep with sand in my hair and salt in my cry.

When I was older he told me I used to do that a lot as a baby, cry. He said it didn't take long to work out I only stopped when I was in water. In the bath, tub, sink, bird fountain, holy water – whatever was around at the time. I'd begin laughing, he reckoned, become a different kid. But when they took me away from it again I'd start crying, wriggling and flapping my limbs.

Just like a fish outta water, he said.

And music, he said, he'd play me hymns on the radio and sometimes on the organ and I'd rock back and forth to hits like 'Breath of God' and 'The Holy City', and 'Joyful Joyful'. When I got older he showed me which fingers to stick on which keys to play notes on that organ. I was getting good until the day one of the young churchgoers from the local parish came in and did a solo concert for us orphans on his guitar. What was this thing of beauty? That acoustic was more organic than the sound of falling water. Father O must've seen me all wide-eyed and silent and figured a guitar was more portable than a piano and he gave the guy five bucks a pop to visit me once a week and teach me the chords.

I'd found my oasis on land.

And I got good at it.

So good that before I was eight I was accompanying Father O on Sunday mornings up next door at the Catholic Church. Not many people attended in our community so he didn't take it seriously and I didn't get nervous. He'd belt out the hymns on the ivories while I'd play the rhythm. Sometimes he'd turn to look across at me and he'd wink, or nod, and we'd become even more symbiotic, and I would strum a little harder or concentrate more. And I think the few attendees liked seeing the cute kid with chocolate eyes beneath a nest of hair struggling to hold the giant borrowed guitar.

'Joyful Joyful' never sounded more joyful.

After a while more people started turning up and within a couple of months there was standing room only. I got more confident. I even started singing a bit, joining in with the chorus or helping with harmony, until Father O put a microphone in front of me one day and I closed my eyes and sang three songs in a row. Afterwards I opened them again and he led the assembly in a rousing applause.

They didn't come here to listen to God, he told me afterwards, just you.

I'M COMING WITH YOU

Witi's mum hadn't handled his dad's disappearance well. Sure, she seemed to be getting better every year, but he had a hunch she was just better at hiding her sadness from him. He'd hear later about people losing years in a matter of weeks when a family member died suddenly. He saw her shoulders droop under the weight and stay there. She stopped functioning at her admin job in the accountancy office and ended up behind a sewing machine in a building full of duplicate sewers. Her friends dwindled from many to only a couple of hard-core mates who could handle her stress. She didn't talk much and sometimes he'd catch her sitting and staring. Especially at the old landline that never rang. Their garden grew heaps of weeds and when a new spring season came around Witi would see his mum unsure what to do with the warmth.

Still, of all the things she lost, being his mum wasn't one of them. He felt her protection every day, from the first day his dad left. A year later she must've got determined not to let him become as insular and lost as she was, because visits to Dr Herbert suddenly became a weekly thing. It felt like a million visits. Finally, when she attended one time, his mum saw the look in Witi's eyes and heard the deadpan answers and she realised something was dying inside her son – so she decided to protect Witi from psychological interference as well.

Always protective. Recently Witi joked the new iPhone in his pocket would achieve the same thing. She took hold of his shoulders and just stared at him for him a bit, like she'd seen a new piece of his dad in his face. She kissed his forehead and broke the moment with a wisecrack: Thank God you don't have a receding hairline like he does.

Like he does ...

Yeah nah, she was still talking about Dad in the present. As if he could walk through the front door at any time.

Next morning his mum lit a single candle on the breakfast table. But neither of them said anything about it being the anniversary of the day his dad disappeared. After Witi rinsed his plate he placed a hand on her shoulder. She put both of hers on top of his and gave a nod.

Witi ignored the turn-off to college. Instead he drove through the suburban streets that snaked towards the main artery. Slowing at one of the last intersections, he saw Alana. He stopped and she ran around the side of the car. Her smile said she'd been there a while.

She slammed the passenger door shut and gave a deep, excited sigh.

I wasn't sure you'd take this route, she said. Almost gave up.

Whaddya even doing here? he asked. You should be at school.

Yet here we are.

But I'm heading out to the coast.

I know. I'm coming with you.

He looked in the rear-view mirror at the cars backing up behind them. I'm not going surfing, he said, and I'm not looking for company. Not today. It's sort of …

Personal?

Complex.

C'mon, Witi, I'm sick of being your rehab friend, always picking up the pieces while you get over it. Don't turn into your mum.

He imagined his mum sitting behind her sewing machine, surrounded by co-workers who couldn't give a shit about her problems. He thought of the brave face she'd put on in the smoko room, and the fact she still had to pump out her quota for the day, while he bailed on all responsibilities.

The first car honk from behind them brought Witi back to Alana.

Just drive. Please?

Fine, he said.

They headed north, up over the steep, thin road that wove over the Remutaka ridgeline. Alana insisted they park up at the summit for a few minutes, and with their home turf stretching in the distance behind them, she made him lean in while she took a selfie. After deciding his grimace wasn't worth keeping, she kissed his cheek on the second go, and captured his smile with a well-timed digital chime.

Down the other side and onto the flats, they headed east into deep farmland where the paddocks grew steeper and higher. Around each blind corner they were greeted with another patchwork of fencing and pockets of sheep and cattle, and trees that grew buckled towards the coast due to the prevailing wind.

Alana finally asked where they were going.

Witi didn't answer.

At the peak they could just make out a slice of dark green sparkling on the horizon, but before she got too excited about being close, they twisted down another hill that buried them deep in a valley of forestry. The tar seal gave way to loose gravel, and a thick tail of dust rose behind them. At the end of a minor incline the sea seemed to rush up to meet them. The road turned sharp right and began flirting with the foreshore and its white surges of water across shiny black stones.

Witi stopped the car. He drew up the zip on his top, pulled its hood over his head, and got out. Just above the tide mark, he crouched and leant his back against a large rock. He stared at the small waves peeling along the reef and after a while he felt Alana sit quietly beside him.

They listened to the hiss of water as it pushed back and forth across the stones. In past trips Witi had to hitch to the coast and hike the rest of the way. His time here would be short – never enough to let a year's worth of build-up blow out to sea – but it was still way better than going through the day surrounded by concrete and technology and the 'bad' positive ions they generated. The ocean, on the other hand, was full of the good stuff, the negative ions. Witi figured that the rationale for this was science having a crack at humour. A real stitch-up. Whatever, Physics reckoned the foreshore was the best place to clear an injured soul. So each anniversary he came.

Or perhaps the horizon represented hope of a new beginning?

It didn't help that he felt Alana was trying to tune into his thoughts the whole time. Little noises came from her, like she was searching for a reason to say something. In the end she must've given up because the best she could do was sync her breathing with his.

Later he heard her say his name, sort of dreamy, but clear as.

Yeah?

I didn't say anything, she replied.

You said my ... nah nuthin'. Must be hearin' things.

And the ocean called his name again.

You would've liked Father O, pal.

He was two people in the one body. Not that he had two heads, but he could've. He had two parts to the brain, one left, one right, and it was easy to work out which one he was talking to you with. Not that I ever heard him use the other half with anyone else but me.

You should always try and exercise both sides of your brain, he'd say.

Yeah, you would've liked him a lot.

I was his favourite. Father O'Reilly was his real name but I just called him Father O. He didn't care, so the other orphans called him that too and it stuck. Father O liked the symbolism that a full circle represented. Two parts joining in the middle, he'd say, and one part of his brain would say:

God uses the circle as a symbol of all things eternal and there is none more creative than He.

While the other part of his brain would say something like ... actually, pal, you'd have to understand Father O's life before the clergy to know what he'd say.

Father O wasn't one of us.

He was from Northern Ireland. Raised as a Catholic into a world of religious conflict, he turned to rock music and surfing to escape the violence on the streets. During a solo surf in the giant waves below the Cliffs of Moher a light appeared on the end of Father O's surf-board, perfectly framed by the oval opening at the end of the tube, and it told him he had to travel to the bottom of the Earth to prepare for an arrival of great significance. Afterwards he sat on the beach and concluded it couldn't have been anything else.

He figured God must surf.

This is good news, pal.

This is when he started using the other part of his brain. He trained to be a priest, made his pilgrimage to the Southern Hemisphere and waited.

And waited

And waited

Until I turned up at the front door like a piece of driftwood with the ocean in my eyes.

He never lost that other part of his brain, the one he had before sharing a barrel with the Big Fullah. Father O told me once he didn't believe he was chosen because he was some sort of pure soul or anything (cos he reckoned he was a bit of a hell-raiser as a kid), but because of who he was before that wave. For a reason. What reason, neither part of his brain actually bothered to tell me. Or never got a chance to. Whatever. So he did what he believed was best for me.

When I was two he took me to the beach and as I laughed in the shore break he witnessed the waves fall on me, push me over, then help me back to my feet. Like the ocean was as young and playful as

I was. He heard me speak to the ocean and he was convinced that in some silent way it spoke back.

He kept a couple of old surfboards tucked under a stack of pews behind the confession booth, so he took one down to the beach and waded out to deep water and watched from his board as a wave appeared and nudged me safely back to the beach while I stared at my feet so steady above the ocean's surface.

Again and again.

Never once falling.

He knew the ocean would never drown me.

He kept the religious part of his brain for everyone else and dedicated this other part to me.

Some Sundays he'd keep the sermon short in order to catch the surf before the ten-thirty onshore appeared, and he'd usher people away early with God's blessing.

He said he never taught me to surf because you can't teach what's already known.

So each year he and I rode the waves together

    Small days

    Big days

At local and remote breaks

Amongst heavy crowds and sometimes just the two of us.

I spoke to the swell and it answered me with set waves and the deepest barrels.

And inside each oval cavity I saw infinite energy and felt it absorbed into my skin. And heard the voices.

I saw what other surfers couldn't see.

I heard what others surfers couldn't hear.

Father O said, What sort of boy is this, that even wind and sea obey him?

One day I asked him who my parents were.

But he reckoned I came from the ocean, and I figured he was right.

Yeah, pal, you would've liked him.

But my part of his brain hadn't finished with me.

One night when I was eight, Father O came into my bedroom and woke me up.

Come, chap, he said, it's time.

His breath smelt and he walked with a funny step, but it was late and I wasn't completely awake. He took me to our church. He never turned on the lights and in the darkness our footsteps sounded like gunshots. I watched as he got a chair and reached up to open a manhole in the roof. He brought down a bag, then he lit a couple of candles while I sat on the front-row pew and dangled my feet.

He sat and rummaged through the bag, finally letting out an *Aaaah* when he found what he was looking for. It was a vinyl record – one of the first, I reckon, from the worn state of it. He twirled the cover on its corners and stared at the back.

You know, in some cultures music is the religion, he said. Makes it all simple, doesn't it? No God, no church, no – he looked around and swung a drunken hand – this. Just music. Worse ways to live your life, huh? I mean, who really knows, lad? It's all just one big unknown. Interpretation. That's what it comes down to. No wonder we fight over it. But music ... we all understand that. You know? Course you bloody know, 'cos you're the special one.

He took a black disc out of the cardboard sheath and got up from his chair.

The church had an old record player and in the stillness of the room I heard static from the speakers and the pulse of the needle in the outside groove.

Me and Pink Floyd were like this back in the day, he said, showing me his crossed fingers in the orange glow of the flames. The church began filling with the sound of bleeps and synthesiser.

Floyd, this is the special one, he yelled over it. He held his hands to me, then waved them at the sound.

Special one, Floyd.

He sat beside me as shadows from the candles danced on the walls around us.

Led Zep IV
A Night at the Opera
LA Woman
Madman across the Water
Sgt Pepper

I met them all that night and others too. And heard how each one shaped Father O's life in some way. How they gave him inspiration. A doorway out of chaos.

By the end of the last album I still hadn't moved. I heard the arm lift on the record player and the church went silent again, except for the snoring from Father O next to me. I needed to wee. I stood and crept past him as the first light was spreading through the stained-glass window.

I'm going to fail yo -u if you don't show me, he mumbled to someone in his sleep.

WHEN YOU'RE TEN EVERYTHING'S TRUE

Witi only heard his name called twice. He sensed a flashback, like a once-familiar song or a smell that takes you back in time, to another place. His dad. Dr Herbert's fake-sympathetic voice and the stench of stale cigars. It was unsettling so he tried to wash it away with conversation:

Me and the old man came here once, he told Alana.

He showed her the place where his dad had lit a small fire so they could warm themselves. It was higher up the beach, near where the land rose sharply and soared skywards, covered in native bush. Back then, his dad had pointed out to him the two peaks further down the coast, their outline a couple of heads staring out at the horizon. He told Witi about his mum's whakapapa connection to this land and the strictly tapu caves up there that still held noble remains from centuries past.

Your ancestral Kaumatua, he'd told Witi. Part of her, part of you.

The two heads were said to be twins who were in love with the same girl, Witi now told Alana. When both brothers refused to leave, she learnt of their battle for her heart, and when she couldn't persuade them to stop fighting, she couldn't bear to stay. She took a waka and paddled out to where the sea meets the sky. The brothers stood shoulder to shoulder and waited for her return, each refusing to give up before the other.

I guess they're still waiting for her, huh? Witi said. That's women for ya.

Alana stared at the landscape in awe. Is it true?

When you're ten everything's true.

I meant the caves.

Yeah. Mum reckons they're sacred-as. She said there're heaps of stories like that going way back.

He reached into his t-shirt and pulled out a small bone carving; he presented it in his open palm.

Even the old man was into it, collecting stuff like this old thing.

Alana took care lifting it; her fingers massaged the smooth curves and for a moment she and it seemed to leave Witi.

When did you get this?

Eight years ago. Today. Here. The old man's final act to his son.

It's beautiful.

It's pointless, that's what it is.

Alana's brown eyes lifted to his. That why I've never seen it?

He shrugged.

You're such an egg, Witi. He must've told you something about it? What about these markings? That face? The holes?

The sun and ocean. Stepping in and out of doors or a door. Or somethin'. Dunno what. It sounded like too much responsibility at the time. He wore one too, the exact other half of this. He showed me how they fitted together to form the one big one. I can still picture a glow in my head if I think about that moment.

He took it back from her. He'd said too much. Alana was always digging, looking for understanding – she'd make a good cop one day – and he couldn't be bothered with questions he didn't know the answers to.

Hey, yeah nah, probably just a kid seeing things, eh, he said.

He knew she'd come back to it. He sensed if she could understand this relic, then perhaps she could do the same to him.

Later, they sat on the bonnet of the car. Witi wrote prose in his notebook while she rested her head on his shoulder – and continued romanticising about his ancestors. But he wasn't really listening. He was watching the thin line of cloud fixed to the horizon and wondering whether it was the first sign of the cyclone arriving, like the furthest circular line on the TV weather guy's map.

The days before his dad vanished Witi found bits of cut-out newspaper nicely arranged on the kitchen table. He started shuffling through them randomly, but when his old man entered the room he went spaz, so Witi opened the front door to escape. A gust of wind blew in and scattered them across the room. He watched his dad on his hands and knees trying to put them back in some order between f-bombs and sharp mumbles and Witi wondered what the big deal was. They were just stupid scraps of newsprint.

A few years later, when Witi could stand on tiptoes and blindly reach a top shelf in one of their cupboards, he knocked a manila folder to the ground and the same pieces of paper spewed out. Puzzled again, he leafed through the three weeks' worth of isobar maps from the weather section of their local newspaper.

He put the notebook down on the bonnet and picked up the guitar. Lightly fingering the strings and shifting from one chord to another, he brought the words to life. When he paused to review a line, Alana told him she'd heard her parents talking about the prospect of the packhouse shutting down due to the recession, and their jobs becoming redundant. Arguments had started in her home. Her dad wanted them to head north to some bigger smoke with more opportunities and a caravan in the backyard of an uncle's place. Her mum wanted to head across town to another packhouse and try their luck. Alana couldn't tell what that would mean for her. Or for their friendship.

She suggested Witi change a lyric and he did.

On the drive home Witi told Alana that the band for the college dance on Saturday night had pulled out. Mr Mullen from music had volunteered him to stand in.

Why didn't you tell me earlier? That's awesome news.

Dunno, wasn't sure if I should take him up.

You're gonna do it though, eh?

He seems to think I've got the goods.

You've got the pedigree.

Witi scoffed. I'm a busker compared to what Dad achieved. He was touring the country at our age.

I've heard his music. You're better than he was.

Spoken like a natural agent.

More like groupie.

Careful, the old man married one of those.

There was never going to be anyone else but your mother, pal.

Me and her met at a gig at a local pub in Wellington. This small smoky joint downstairs from the main street. It was a popular place for young people and the owner, Charlie, carved a reputation as someone who liked to party with his punters, often for the right reasons, other times for his own. Yeah, mostly for his own.

Charlie used to tell everyone he discovered me first, even before Father O. I remember how he walked past me when I was busking that day on the street; he had the heaviest shoulders I'd seen. He stopped and just stared at me and each time I looked at him his body seemed to straighten a little bit more. Nothing weird there, people did it all the time with me. Four songs later, he asked me how old I was and didn't flinch when I told him I was seventeen. He asked if I'd be interested in playing in his club three nights a week. No pay up front, but I'd get food and drink, which considering the hardship I was in sounded better than living on the sound of coins falling in a case.

The first Friday night I played I found out why he'd been so down. I sang for three hours to just four people and the bar lady.

But the next night those four brought another four.

The following Thursday those four brought a few more friends.

Then on the Friday those friends brought other friends.

And for Saturday night the place was full.

Within two months Charlie had taken on three new bar staff, two bouncers, and he'd bought himself a new suit to wear amongst the sea of pretty young things who came to listen to me. Soon after, he was asking me to start an hour earlier and finish two hours later.

Two shows a night, he said, clasping me by my cheeks. These kids are so fuckin' into you, man.

He smelt of cigars and he had a new liking for jewellery and aviator sunglasses and he had a habit of picking the best-looking girls to join him in his office above the club during each show. From my spot on stage I got a clear view of their silhouettes behind the frosted glass. But I said yes anyway. And he rewarded me by pressing a roll of cash into my jeans pockets.

Get some new clothes, would ya? Those are ripped and that t-shirt smells like shit and those jandals are not cool. And for chrissakes get a bloody haircut — you look like a fuckin' surf bum.

With a pocket full of cash I walked out that door and bought my first new surfboard.

There was no shortage of girls in that place.

They probably thought they had a front row to the entertainment when they bunched up at the stage and danced and sang, but as a seventeen-year-old male, I was definitely the one in the front row. They were into my t-shirt that smelled like shit and ripped jeans and long hair still damp from the surf an hour earlier. Yeah, there were

offers and invitations from them, all sorts of invitations and offers.
But I was now a professional musician and getting better at it. I was
seventeen and hungry. Your mother will tell you I couldn't communicate with girls, that I was a mute, with the world's smallest vocabu-
lary outside of singing, but I could communicate through music and
surfing very well. Without these though, pal, I was hopeless.

A fish outta water, Father O would've said.

Your mum had eyes like

> Moonlight riding a midnight wave
>
> Easterly sun greeting a westerly wave
>
> Rainbow circles in the spray sent from a wave

And they stared at me from amongst the sea of dead faces.

And I stared back.

She came each Thursday night for a month. Then most Fridays too.
Then come Saturdays she was there again in the front row staring at
me from amongst the dead faces.

And still I stared back.

Others had eyes for her; I saw them from my spot up on stage, trying
to slide into her life with offers of drinks and invitations to get better
acquainted. She was a stunner, your mother, but she didn't abuse it
like those other girls who thought the rest of the world was watching
while they seduced the dance floor and sent me offers and invita-

tions and eventually disappeared behind Charlie's office door where in my peripheral I watched them perform through the frosted glass.

Nah, your mother only had eyes for me.

Yeah, she reckoned it took three months before we spoke our first words to each other, but she was wrong – I'd been communicating with her from that very first night.

She just didn't know it.

My first words to her were an apology and they came during a typical night in the club. I was halfway through the second set when Charlie started circling the dance floor in his white suit and aviators with a couple of pre-mix bottles in each hand – the sweet potent stuff he liked to use for bait. It was a busy evening and he had the pick of the floor, but for me only one pair of eyes stood out.

Like luminescent algae glowing in the night surf.

I watched Charlie enter the mass of bodies, silent and still-faced, squeezing through couples and groups, barely acknowledging the locals and invitations and offers. He wandered the floor like this for a while before he made a cut through the bodies and stopped at your mother.

Do you want a drink?

No, thanks.

No, seriously, it's on the house – I own the place.

Thanks, but no.

Would you like something else? I have more this way.

I'm okay.

What's your name?

(Indecipherable)

You're very pretty.

(Silence)

(Pointing) Why don't we head up to my office for a while? It has a great view.

Here's fine.

Charlie's hand travelled down her back and when it stopped on her ass the look she gave me felt like a ten-foot shore dump to my head.

I dropped my guitar and dived off the stage, throttling Charlie in a tackle that made a crater amongst the crowd. His aviators skittered across the floor and were smashed in the panic of feet. Charlie's hands grabbed my throat and he squeezed until my body screamed for oxygen. I only threw one punch that night but it was enough to draw blood above his eye. I would've got in another one if his two bouncers hadn't lifted me above their heads and carried me out.

Charlie was yelling all sorts of threats, said I wouldn't work there again and I was a dime a dozen and I was just a fuckin' useless surf bum and I had to pay for the dry-cleaning bill to get the blood out of his suit.

But he was a molesting fuckin' predator.

It hurt when I hit the concrete outside. It also hurt when they threw my guitar out the door after me and it landed on my head. I stood, picked it up, and when I turned your mum was there, standing toe to toe with me. She held my hand and kissed my lips and I thought this was the best day of my life. She opened her eyes and I instantly fell into the green ocean. I've been swimming in it ever since.

Sorry if my t-shirt smells like shit.

But we were interrupted by a man in a smart suit.

He said he'd heard about me from some people in the know and had come down to check me out for himself and was very, very impressed with what he'd heard, despite the little altercation. He pulled out a shiny steel container with a flip-top lid and handed me the whitest card with fancy gold writing:

Randy Richman, Oval Records

You need to come downtown in the morning, he said. I've got some influential people who'd like to meet you. Make sure you do, okay?

I nodded.

He turned to your mother. If you care about this guy, you'll make sure he does.

She nodded.

He began walking away and was smothered by the shadows.

They're gonna fuckin' love you! he called back.

DISTURBING THE YEARS OF PEACE

Jordy wanted to come home with Witi the next afternoon. He was still having trouble making friends around college after his grand entrance on the first day, and the swell had disappeared, so he reckoned Witi was his next best thing. Witi tried to tell him it wasn't worth the trip; his place was just like any other three-bedroom, single-parent, weatherboard house in the Valley. But Alana, who was sitting next to them, added that his pad had a pretty cool shrine in it.

You're not Buddhist, are ya? Jordy asked.

Witi flinched his eyes at Alana.

Actually, she added, shaking her head, it's just some old boards and stuff, probably nothing an Aussie like you wouldn't have seen a hundred times.

Nah, too easy. I'm in.

Witi stewed on it for the rest of the afternoon. Hosting was not exactly his forte. It didn't help that Jordy had asked to be a friend and to follow Witi on every social media platform he was on, even the ones he didn't use anymore. Real stalker-like. Witi decided it would be easier to bail before the end of school and make some excuse the next time he saw Jordy. So in the last class of the day, during a video on scientists' warnings of more intense weather patterns due to climate change, he faked a coughing frenzy, excused himself a couple of minutes early, hurried through the hall towards the exit, and sprinted across the open space of the rugby field. But when Witi got to his car, Jordy was already leaning against it, waiting.

You got off early too, huh? he said. Mate, what's the chances?

Witi unlocked the vehicle and Jordy called shotgun.

Witi offered him a cheese and Marmite sandwich. They ate them on the back deck overlooking the railway line dissecting the yard from the neighbour's. Jordy took large bites and when he spoke he packed it all to one side of his mouth. They talked surfing, mainly. He didn't seem to have a problem letting Witi know about his conquests: six-foot Noosa for a full month three years back, road trips to Supertubes, camping along the New South Wales coast, surfing and shagging his way from Ballina to Bondi and back again, tow-in sessions at an outer reef somewhere west where if the crazy hold-down from the wave didn't get you then the sharks would, and if they didn't, then the locals would give you a hiding simply because you survived. There was more, but Witi struggled to take it all in. Jordy had packed a lot of crap into eighteen years and it sounded too hardcore to be kosher. Until Jordy pulled the latest iPhone out of his pocket and started swiping through some photographic proof. How could a kid his age have a piece of tech more expensive than everything in their house combined? He enjoyed Jordy's animations, though: he had thick hands with fingers that flexed like a pro wrestler as he re-enacted scenes full of tubes, tits and fists.

Played a heap of footie too. Made a few state teams. So you do anything else other than surf? he asked Witi. Rugby? Soccer? Cricket? Farkin' netball?

Nah, not too good on land eh. Witi looked at his hands like he had a disability. These things are only good at catching waves.

Witi went inside to get them a drink and when he came back he found Jordy bent over with his jeans around his ankles and his ass exposed to the passengers of the three fifty-five train as it sped past. He looked up at Witi with a smile like it was the most fun he'd had all year.

Jordy eventually asked about the shrine.

C'mon mate. What was ya missus talking about?

She's not. We're not ... Witi struggled to find the right wording. He liked how Jordy made it sound and didn't want to break the illusion. And there was a natural urge to protect his patch anyway. But Jordy wasn't waiting.

Orgh, you're stuck in the friend-zone, eh? Ruined a tonne of farkin' good blokes, that has.

There was no way out of the situation, so Witi took him to the shed, reached behind a brick amongst the weeds, and retrieved the key. He'd considered asking Jordy to turn away for a sec, but it was weird to think that the only Aussie fullah in college would ever rip him off. And while he might spit bits of bread when he talked, his personality seemed honest enough.

Witi kicked its base and the door opened.

He brushed cobwebs from the light switch and turned it on. Two fluorescent bulbs coughed in the darkness before humming to life. The first row of stacked surfboards appeared, still organised in small to tallest. The other row, double in size, sat crammed in the opposite wall. Part of the drum kit filled a corner, while two giant speakers, one on its side, sat in silence beside it. There was the record player, CD player, recording device, microphones, all stacked on top of the amplifier, and a mess of colourful cords running back and forth like a multi-laned expressway on the concrete floor. The guitar stand sat empty next to two carpenter's horses wrapped in soft fabric. The tins of resin and sheets of fibreglass and an old builder's plane were corralled in the corner of a workshop bench. Yellow-tinged posters of surfing and girls, from the nineties for the most part, hung in prominent places. On some the Blue-Tack had weathered and their top halves had collapsed like they'd got too tired waiting for someone to walk through the door and appreciate them. Each of Jordy's footsteps felt like they were disturbing years of peace.

Jesus, he said, what *is* this place?

The old man's stuff.

Who are ya? Jack Johnson's son?

Witi stood near the door, wary that each step he took inside would be further reason for Jordy to take his time. So he watched him orbit the room and take it all in. Witi waited for the real question, but it didn't come straight away. Instead Jordy fingered each board, sporadically pulling individual ones out from their rack to check their lines and weight and to read the dimensions tattooed along their stringers. He commented where he could: this one was like his first board, while that one would rip in small waves; these two were in awesome nick for something so retro. Hell, they *all* were ...

At one stage he bumped the drum-kit cymbals, but caught them before they hit the ground. He found a drumstick amongst the rubble and began lightly tapping on the cymbals, sending a sparkly tone into the puffs of dust and for a second Witi felt the old shed stir. Jordy turned to Witi with a smile and continued, still tapping the stick on anything hard, including the length of an old church pew. He paused beside the large framed picture and drew the palm of his hand across the grime on the glass. Each swipe gave him reason to make another until he had exposed the image of a guy saturated in stage lights and sex appeal, frozen in demigod pose.

Who's this dude?

My dad.

Must've been some sorta legend, huh?

And that's when he asked it:

Where's he now?

I should've known better than to trust another guy in a suit, pal.

The Oval Records office was all shiny Italian suits and shiny wooden flooring and shiny sterling-silver business card holders and the people I was introduced to all had shiny rings and shiny black shoes.

The fattest one told me to sit. Help myself to a mint.

Sweet, nah, I said.

Figured he was the head honcho. The Chief. He gleamed so much, air slid off him.

Well, he said, leaning back in his shiny leather chair, they tell me you can sing and play the guitar. Rodge here says you're the real shit. The next big thing.

Sweet, nah, I said.

We were high up, here in downtown. I reckoned I could see the Bay if I stood. The old orphanage with its boarded-up front door. Or your mother waiting for me on the seat out on the footpath ten floors below.

Someone handed me a guitar.

Play us something, the Chief said, whatever you want.

So I tried something I wrote that morning.

Never even played it before.

They got me a band.

They called us Blackwhole. It's an infusion of nature and sex, Rodge
said.

They got us a manager and sent us around New Zealand a few times.

We played in pubs, then halls, then outdoor venues.

A constant sea of dead faces except for one pair of eyes that stood out
like

Oval cavities of infinite energy.

And when they thought we'd done enough they sent us to Australia
and Britain.

I visited Ireland and the Cliffs of Moher.

I sent Father O and your mother postcards,

Wish you were here, that sorta stuff.

We had internal issues with band members, so the manager left us,
then came back again. They wanted a record from me every year.

It's in the contract you signed, they said.

When did a circle marked in pen become someone's signature?

I dunno, pal, it got tough.

The invitations and offers. Exercising both parts of my brain. Land-
locked in some new town a million miles from the energy source.

People wanted to know what

That song was about

This song was about

Who's the girl I sing about in that song

And is she the same one in the other one

Was I really an orphan

My influences

And so on

Sweet, nah.

I stayed on the tour bus when the others didn't, and when I did leave it I stood with my back glued to the wall and answered nuthin'.

And people began talking, saying I was losing it, that I was sick.

By now I hadn't seen Rodge for years and the record people told me the Chief was playing our music on his superyacht somewhere in the Mediterranean.

I missed Father O. I especially missed your mum. I was being sucked empty and I wanted to get off the ride.

You can't, they said, it's in the contract you signed.

And sucked me some more.

Until I got so sick they finally said they'd stop.

But they didn't.

They released Blackwhole's Greatest Hits.

Just a local tour to promote it, they said, a few familiar places.

But I wasn't well.

Your mother pleaded with the manager to get me help.

Sure, after the tour, luv. Promise.

I stopped getting out of bed

I didn't write anything

I left my guitar in strange places

The bass player said he had better things to do and slammed the door

The drummer got poached by another band

But I still had your mother.

They were forced to cancel the tour and said I was in big trouble.

It got tough, pal

They showed me the contract

And I drew two eyes and an upside down mouth in my circle signature

A lawyer said I'd been mistreated and offered to help

But he sucked what little was left

while I stared at my reflection in his shoes.

I shaved my hair into a Mohawk

And wore undies and a singlet in places I shouldn't

I took a liking to energy drinks and vodka

And paddled out in the ocean in the dark so no one would see me.

I tried to hold a conversation, a simple hello would do

But it didn't recognise me.

They'd sucked me dry.

Like a fish outta water.

So they shredded my contract.

And the next day your mother told me she was pregnant.

HE MESSED UP DAD'S STUFF

Jordy's father had a real job; he was a hotshot international doctor in earth sciences with more letters after his name than Witi had in his own. So many letters, in fact, the New Zealand Government had brought him over to quantify what climate change was doing to the East Coast. So Jordy said, but he was vague and when his eyes drooped Witi could tell Jordy was as bored as he was with the details.

Sounded like they lived in a flash-as house, though.

All the latest stuff in it including a cleaning lady.

Why was he at their school then?

Jordy clasped his hands behind his head, sat back against the wall, and looked crookedly at the seascape painting beside him. It had hung there in the background of Witi's and Mum's lives forever but now Witi was embarrassed how outdated it was.

I've spent my teenage life hopscotching around Australia doing the same thing, Jordy said. Global warming's big business, mate, and not many have the qualifications like my dad. You could say he's the right guy at the right time. The guy's a farkin' genius apparently. Actually I spent a bit of time here in your backyard when I was about eight. I wasn't old enough to remember, though.

You must've seen some different colleges eh?

Jordy twitched fingers. Five, if we include your one.

You don't like boarding schools?

I ain't good at being confined.

Witi looked over at the clock on the oven – his mum would be home shortly and he had this sudden urge to keep Jordy here just to see the look on her face.

You want dinner? he asked.

His eyes fizzed. Sure. What we havin'?

Witi's mum finally arrived home in a clutter of full grocery bags and limbs. She huffed as she juggled to hold, balance, and shut the front door behind her. Jordy was quick to assist, so quick that she assumed it was Witi releasing the bags from her wrist. She let out a shriek and fell back against the wall.

Jesus!

Nah, name's Jordy. Close enough. Here, gimme the rest of those.

She cooked a mean curry sausage dish. Jordy reckoned he'd never had such fat sausages before and she took the credit for it even though all she'd done was pay for them at the local butcher. She did take the credit for the homemade shortbread, though, and when Jordy took his third piece from the plate, she gave Witi a smirk that said she wasn't quite sure what to make of his new friend. She was quick to pick up on Jordy's situation and proceeded to fire questions at him like some sort of security check. Jordy answered as if he had nothing to hide:

Yep, Dad knows where I am. I texted him earlier.

Yeah, he's a doctor, the boffin kind.

Nah, you've gotta be good at science, and I'm a physical education sorta guy.

Mum died a few years back.

Nope, I'm an only lonely. Number one son in a one-son race. I think at some stage they might've tried, but they were both away so often, what's the point, huh? At least this way I only have to watch my own back.

It was about there that Witi brought the interrogation to a close. His mum was enjoying herself, but that last comment was tip-toeing a line that Witi didn't want to be near. For her sake too, despite the fact she probably knew exactly what she was doing and probably wanted to probe a bit more about Jordy's mum's death. That would've struck a chord with her for sure. Witi didn't have a fall-back discussion point to raise, so in the silence he herded shortbread crumbs around the saucer with his finger while she straightened a spoon flush with the patterns on the table. Jordy began tapping eight finger nails on the Formica like a couple of horses galloping.

You guys have a toilet?

Witi and his mum automatically fell into routine: she went for the brush, while he hit the tea towel drawer. Witi knew she wanted to talk about Jordy, but instead they small-talked the usual way for this time of the night, like how the hot tap needed fixing because it was loose as, and what'd Alana been up to.

But as the minutes went by, Witi was getting more conscious of Jordy's non-appearance, and with every dish dried he stared back at the door with a higher expectation of seeing him. Mum was evidently thinking the same because when Witi finally suggested he check she didn't even let him finish his sentence before telling him to go.

The hallway was empty and silent. Witi felt the cold rush of dread when he found the toilet door open, the light still on, and heard the hiss of the reservoir in the final stages of refilling. There were three other doors: one for a cupboard, two for bedrooms. While finding Jordy in either of those would be a kooky enough, it was the room tucked around the corner of the hall that Witi was most concerned about.

But that was where he found him.

You couldn't exactly call it a room, more like some governmental draughtsman's afterthought to fill a corner of a state house as cheaply as possible. Witi's dad had used it to stash his more important personal stuff, like his music awards, photo albums and scrapbooks of album reviews and concert write-ups. It was the only place where he kept his fascination with the coast on show. He displayed his stuff like a museum collection, everything in its place. Maybe he was trying to decipher it, like a TV detective tracking a serial killer. Maps and drawings and bits of cotton wool pinned taut, connecting images and words. It looked like a jumble of nonsense. It might as well've been in some other fuckin' language. German or Portuguese or something, take your pick.

Either way, the room was sacred to Witi and his mum. As far as Witi knew nothing had been disturbed since his dad was last in the house. Early on in the disappearance Witi's mum figured he'd be back shortly and she didn't want to upset him. These days Witi guessed it had kind of become house policy. Maybe if they actually discussed it, they'd see the silliness in it all. Not that he'd want to start that conversation. So for now it was frozen in time, like any of his photos in the family albums.

From the doorway he saw Jordy standing in the corner holding the carved walking stick, running his thumbnail through the grooves and contours of its lines. He held it up to his eye with spread hands and looked down its length like it was a rifle. He swept the end through the air and paused with it pointing at Witi's head.

Bang, he said. His grin in full-on wind-up mode.

What the fuck, man? Witi whispered. Put that down.

Jordy carelessly dropped it back on the sidebar, already picking up a small notebook with the other hand.

You shouldn't be in here, Witi threatened.

Witi, mate, you gave me the cheapo tour. This is what Alana was talking about, eh?

Witi didn't answer. Instead he plucked the notebook from him and gently placed it back. Jordy went to grab the next available thing, like a toddler, but Witi grasped a handful of t-shirt and dragged him back outside the door. He stood in the entrance to keep him out.

Jordy craned over his shoulder.

Bet the answer to your ol' man's disappearance is in there somewhere, he whispered.

We don't need your help, Witi quietly said. He pushed and Jordy staggered back.

They stared at each other. For a second Jordy looked as if he was going to apologise, but more likely he was torn between doing the right thing and seeing how far he could go now that he'd crossed the line. In the silence Witi's hands made fists.

A splinter of light broke through the window and tracked across the wall. It settled bright behind Jordy, making him a silhouette. Suddenly Witi saw his dad's profile standing there, clear as and holding out a hand. Witi put out his open right hand in return. But the light passed, taking the vision with it, and there was Jordy looking at Witi like he was trying to work out a calculus equation on his forehead. Witi's arm was sticking out taut as a rimu branch.

His mum's voice called out from the kitchen. Your father's here, Jordy.

Jordy's eyes lingered on Witi as he stepped backwards.

Be right there, he replied.

Witi stood at the front window and watched the black BMW. It had begun raining and their porch light amplified the drops struggling for grip on the vehicle's sleek curves. When Jordy opened the passenger door, the interior lit up, and between the pulse of the window wipers, Witi saw a middle-aged man with fine facial features and a heavy fringe that rose and swooped back like the guys on those hair-gain bottles. The man peered at their house. He didn't acknowledge Witi or his son now fiddling with his seatbelt. The light died inside and Witi was left looking at the shell paused in their driveway. He pressed his face and hands against the window to see past his reflection but the vehicle reversed, capturing him in its headlights.

He withdrew and the curtain fell back into place. He remained staring at the thirty-year-old tapestry.

Don't be too hard on him, son, his mum said from across the room. You're as unknown to him as he is to you.

He was snooping.

He was just being curious.

He messed up Dad's stuff.

I touch those things every day. The fact he did doesn't change its wairua.

Let me tell you about wairua, pal.

Your Koro says it's the beginning of you, the spirit within you, the flame that burns.

It stays with you, it directs you and influences how others see you.

*Some say it's in your heart only, while others say it runs from every strand of your brown hair
right down to your feet like paddles and
out to the tips of your scoops.*

*You're a vessel and wairua is the force. Without it you are
a still ocean
a flightless toroa
a guitar with no strings.*

When my contract was being shredded, your wairua was already there, pal.

Growing within your mother, and much bigger than a foetus.

Her beautiful wairua protected yours for nine months.

You are one part me, one part your mum. But your wairua is yours and yours alone.

*And when you're gone it will travel north and join us again in Te Po
The land of departed spirits.*

Your mother took me in and cared for me.

She told me I had a beautiful mind.

That Oval Records had blown my candle out.

We used what money I had from my music to buy a car, and our

house from the state department. It was away from

the oceans of dead faces

and people who asked questions and kept my answers

and people with contracts in their hand.

Your mum never wore shiny shoes or shiny jewellery.

She let me walk around the house in my undies

but she said this house is alcohol free

and we weren't to have a television because that just lets everything

back in like a Trojan horse.

Some sly people found our phone number and wanted an exclusive
story

so your mother yanked the cord from the wall and threw the phone
across the room.

She had a friend who knew a builder and he made a shed next to the
house and when your mum led me outside and took her hands away
from my eyes she told me this was my area to do creative stuff in.

I thought it looked like a giant matchbox.

And something inside me sparked.

For the first few months she'd take me to the beach and she and I would sit on the sand. You were there with us, pal, do you remember? I'd rest my hand on her stomach and you could feel me and I could feel you and your wairua inside.

We'd watch the surfers stand on the ocean's surface. They could read the ocean, but that's about it. I used to talk to it and it'd answer me, but truth is, by this time I'd forgotten how. Breathing on land hadn't been an issue for a while now.

I brought your board, she said, It's on the roof.

Sweet, nah.

Next time, eh? she said.

Always was an optimist, pal.

On the way home from the beach one day your mother took a detour and we ended up outside the orphanage and Father O's church. They were having a garage sale, selling everything before the bulldozers came. No one there except for a grey-haired volunteer who didn't recognise me as we passed the tables of religious stuff and furniture. We went out the back and through a garden gate with a broken hinge. There was a small metal fence and half a dozen headstones. I stood in front of one. It was more circular than the others.

That Father O'Reilly's? your mum asked.

First time she'd seen me cry, eh.

Back inside, the church was empty except for the colours from the stained-glass window but I still managed to find something to stand on to reach up to the manhole in the roof.

I felt around in the darkness and smiled when I heard the rustle of plastic.

Your mother said it was the first smile she'd seen me do for ...

Yeah, well, whaddya expect.

We haven't got anything to play these albums on, she said. This is the nineties.

But there was one outside the door for sale.

I sat on the pew while your mum gave the volunteer some money.

And when she turned she saw me trying to work out how I once dangled my feet from only this far up.

You're gonna be six foot too, pal, even taller.

We strapped that pew on the roof racks and the loud noise of the air channelling between it and my surfboard followed us all the way home.

So, sweet.

At night for weeks I'd sit in the far side of the shed on my pew and listen to the record player:

Dark Side of the Moon

Led Zep II

Abbey Road

Rumours

Captain Fantastic.

I met them all again and others too.

Until your mother would come out in her dressing gown and wake me.

But let me tell you about wairua, pal.

Soon.

THERE'S A BUZZ AROUND THE PLACE

His mum's comments about Jordy touching the stuff in the room had hit a soft spot in Witi's subconscious by morning. Almost enough to make him feel bad for the way he'd acted.

Almost.

Then during breakfast he scrapped with himself over whether to tell her about the growing collection of hallucinations and how his dad made a surprise appearance in their hallway.

But that would mean heading back to Dr Herbert's stuffy beige office again:

He'd have to lie on the hard sofa and stare at the fancy framed qualifications hanging on the wall, and smell his last cigar on his clothing,

and listen to his loaded questions in that stupid sympathetic voice

and hear him hastily scribble notes in his notebook

no way they could've been decipherable

so Witi would become more pissed with Dr H wanting to know how he felt about his father and the voids left

and more anxious about what the man was *really* scribbling in that book

and how much longer was he gonna keep Mum sitting in the corner watching him get verbally probed and checking the clock on the wall, afraid she was gonna be late back for work.

So nah, Witi didn't tell her.

Instead, he added it to the mental album of hallucinations over the two years since his last psychologist visit. He was just gonna have to do it tough and try his own self-therapy. Shove *that* in your notebook, dickhead.

At college, Witi headed to the library. Normally, at one particular table on the mezzanine floor, Alana and he would flick through old-school atlases and scour the world for new coasts with the potential for surf. They would pick a random sea-bound country and compete to figure out where the best waves would be found, based on geological aspect and dominant winds, and reef or sand, or resident river mouths. They'd test their theories using Google Earth on the computer next to them, zooming in on images to see if the lines of swell were a reality or a figment of patchy guesswork. The whole process was a form of escapism and often the morning bell would be nothing more than background noise as they landed on the runway in some exotic location.

Jordy was sitting with her when he arrived. The corner of the small table did its best to separate them as they both leaned and he talked. Jordy had a paper plane in his hand; he pinched along one of its folds repeatedly with his fingernail. Alana threw her head back and laughed at something he said, and suddenly Jordy was laughing too. When Jordy saw Witi, he stopped.

There he is! He lobbed the dart towards him. It glided through the space between them, bounced off Witi's head and tumbled to his feet.

Jordy raised his hands triumphantly. Crash and burn, baby!

Alana tried to hide her laughter.

Witi dropped his bag off his shoulder and swung it into the table leg. He collapsed onto the remaining seat, stretched his legs out, and slid his hands into his pockets.

What's happenin'? he pried.

Your mum's never cooked *me* sausages.

He motioned to Jordy. What'd you tell her?

It was a great meal, mate, he said.

And?

It was great. Truly. Should do it again soon.

Yeah, nah, yeah.

You should try her chicken burgers, Alana said.

I bet she does a good Italian too.

Linguini to die for.

Roasts?

She closed her eyes. Good Lord.

Witi felt his skin tightening. They were having too much fun at his expense. It wasn't how things worked with him and Alana. She was his safe place, a sanctuary in this crazy turd-hole, and Jordy was infiltrating it. But Witi smiled anyway to let them know it was fine, whatever man, and thankfully they moved on.

Jordy said he heard that Witi would be the main event at Saturday's dance. Witi shrugged, it was no big deal. But Alana told Jordy he was as good as he was modest. Jordy confessed that he once learnt to play the start of a Cold Chisel song but that was back in primary school and he doubted its sexual cred around the bonfire anyway. He played an invisible guitar and gave Witi a wink.

Witi didn't fall for it.

That's an image invented by Coke, Witi said. Guys are too busy playing to score girls.

Bullshit. Slick-lookin' dude like yourself. Fingers playing the dames 'round here like a brown Ed Sheeran. Hell, betcha got a silky voice to match.

You're full of it, bro.

How do you think I knew you'd be playing? People are talkin'. For a recluse you're a popular guy with a certain gender demographic at this place.

Witi looked at Alana from under his brow – she was rolling her eyes – then back to Jordy.

Was it good or bad?

You got security yet?

Pfft.

Serious. There's a buzz around the place.

Are you going? Alana asked Jordy.

Dancing? Me?

Yeah.

Jordy became distant and shook his head – Witi would be lying if he didn't loosen up a bit with that response. Obviously dingo didn't dance.

Come, she said to Jordy. With me. Apparently this guy's stuck up onstage hypnotising all the screaming wide-eyed beauties with his fingers anyway so you could save me the embarrassment of heading along by myself.

Jordy looked sideways at Witi who instantly knew that with only himself standing in Jordy's way it wouldn't be enough to turn her down.

When Witi was just four years old his dad took him busking on Cuba Street for the first time. Witi kept an irregular beat with a wooden spoon and a bongo drum amongst the business folk heading home and the excited hum of another Friday night beginning. The next year he progressed to a xylophone with only six keys. His dad would wear a wide-brimmed hat and sunglasses so no one recognised him. And they never played the stuff his dad wrote himself or songs that had made him famous. Instead they covered the guys his dad considered cool. Simple names like Plant, Tull, Petty, Springsteen and Seger. Some people would cross the street to get closer while others would stop and listen from a distance. They would clap or tap their thighs or nod their heads, enchanted by the musician and the cute kid with chocolate eyes beneath a nest of hair. His dad reckoned it took strangers back to a time when moments like this were in abundance in their lives and there was something priceless about that. Sometimes he'd turn to look down at Witi and behind the tint he'd wink, or nod, and they'd become even more symbiotic. Witi would bang the bongo harder or concentrate more on the keys. During each session his dad would take the time to introduce Witi to the crowd, and amongst the clapping Witi would wink and nod in return.

In hindsight, Witi doubted his dad craved the extra fame. And from what he remembered, anything that was tossed in the guitar case was shared amongst the homeless on the way out, so it wasn't about the money. He doubted, too, that it was because his dad enjoyed the look on his mum's face when he and Witi left on a Friday to roam the streets. He figured it was just his dad's way of spreading joy. His place of escape. Creating energy from nothing on the street, or absorbing it in the ocean – that was when he was at his happiest.

RISKY MOVE IN THIS CROWD

Witi can say that now with some sense of confidence.

Saturday's dance started with him staring out at the whole senior school soaked in lights that rained every colour from the roof. Everyone looked so different dressed in their best. His mum had helped him pick a tie and as she left she commented on how handsome he looked and while he chucked it off at the time, as soon as she was behind the closed front door he took another geeze at himself in the window reflection – he tightened his chest behind his best white shirt and turned for a side profile. For the first time he thought she was right. He couldn't wait for Alana to see him.

But Witi soon learnt that everyone here was handsome. The guys had crossed the divide from young adult to manhood, and the girls looked stunning in their lipstick and heels with specks of glitter in their neat hair. They'd become porcelain dolls, beautiful and mysterious.

Witi stepped forward to the microphone.

Good evening.

Play some Blackwhole!

Yeah, nah ... but thanks.

Always someone in the crowd, eh.

Witi began strumming his guitar, and its sound and his voice hummed through the hall. The first of the students responded in pairs or small groups and he watched their steps became quicker, lighter and more joyous as they moved to the music. Riding waves of sound. Surfing in groups. Pockets of party waves. A new alertness filled the dead spaces of the building and by the end of the first chorus no one was left standing still. One giant party wave.

Witi was safe up there on stage. He was in control. Not just of them, but of himself. He was safe behind his wall of music notes and tabs and lines of prose that had no meaning to those on the outside, and an acoustic guitar plugged into a hundred decibels of bliss. His opening song, an original, never heard in public before, with killer riffs. Risky move in this crowd, but he felt untouchable.

Third chorus, second line break, he tore at his tie and it dropped to the floor.

Next gap, between

(G chord) *lightness comes before her* ...

and

(E chord) *she's mine now at 10 a.m.* ...

he tore at his buttons and exposed his favourite t-shirt,

a black *Cream* t-shirt.

A middle finger to the person who drove his body any other time. He'd left. Witi preferred this person here on stage. He was a system of energy. Sending sound waves into the world.

He too was at his happiest.

Alana was up near the stage in her own space. Kind of on her own peak. Witi watched her, barefoot and circling on her toes as she swayed her hips deeply in sync with her hands which snaked and danced between themselves. He waited for her to open her eyes, so he could acknowledge her for the evening, but she never did. So he closed his own eyes and for the next bridge sang deeper into the mic, knowing that him and her were sharing something more intimate than anyone else in the room. He was the wave and she was riding him. The source. With killer riffs. When he opened his eyes she had a smile of delight. It stayed with her for the next four songs including his best Bowie cover.

Jordy had been true to his word and as far as Witi could tell from up on stage had sat out pretty much every opportunity to dance. He hadn't even bothered to find a suit, unlike the other guys in the room. He'd settled for jeans and a floral shirt that became illuminated when certain lights found him. Witi expected him to finally get bored and offend someone. But Jordy looked a little lost amongst the glamour. That was until Witi watched Alana dance her way through the floor, find and negotiate with him, then lead him by the hand back to where she'd started. Here she attempted to jumpstart his dance floor mojo. Witi was happy when Jordy raised his hands, shook his head and tried to tell her something over his music.

Dingo can't dance, Witi thought.

She put her hand up to her ear, so Jordy yelled it again:

He said dingo can't dance!

Alana pulled Jordy closer. He reciprocated. And before Witi knew it they were touching all over the place. And moving in time with each other. And Jordy was smiling, like he was holding the winning lotto ticket. Even up at Witi at one point, making him stumble through a line of lyrics. When some of the punters looked up from their little groups, Jordy feasted on it. He sent Alana in a twirl underneath his hand to provoke Witi further. Once, twice, three times Witi saw her laughter as she spun. Jordy had just trumped any thrill Witi had earned from his earlier songs with the world's most clichéd dance step.

Damn dingo got moves.

So Witi looked away, in time to see the rugby guys and their partners arrive from their pre-dance drink session. They were celebrating making it past the dignitaries at the entrance, avoiding the shame of denial and an unwanted meeting with the principal on Monday morning. Merging instead in a boozy communal hug then moved onto the dance floor. At the front of the stage some of the group broke away and pretended to head bang, raising their hands with horned fingers while their tongues hung like wet towels. The girls formed their own circle, a perfect barrier for sharing the flask of whatever they had. The whole crew's movement was in such contrast to the rest of the students it was like watching a back-surge wave clash with the incoming tide.

All except one dude.

Principal's son, Jimmy, stood motionless in the centre of it all. His chest seemed extra buff, his shoulders squarer, and the stare he was giving Jordy's back was every bit as firm. He looked like the Terminator in a hired suit.

Jordy never saw it coming.

But Witi did.

It happened quick, real quick. Freakin' fast.

Jimmy casually walked up to Jordy, said something, and before Jordy had a chance to turn around and focus on a face, Jimmy's first punch hit its target. Jordy's head snapped back and his legs buckled. He lay motionless on the keyhole line of the basketball court. Alana pushed back at Jimmy, but he went in and threw a kick into Jordy's stomach. Jordy rolled onto his front and tucked his knees under his arms. He coughed and grimaced, trying to find his breath and an arm to rest on. Alana went down to his side and Jimmy stood above them pointing a finger and yelling until the veins on his neck went a deep purple. When Jimmy turned back around to his mates they slapped his shoulder and gave high fives and gestured crudely at Jordy. Fuck 'im, things like that.

But Jordy didn't stay down. He ran into Jimmy with so much force he took out three of his mates who each set off their own domino effect amongst the other students. Suddenly there were bodies horizontal everywhere.

And Witi was providing the soundtrack.

And a cover from the teachers and other adults hanging around the punch and club sandwiches.

His fingers ignoring the scene. Ten professionals here to do a job. Killer riffs, man.

Jordy and Jimmy wrestled briefly on the floor before getting to their feet and in a violent storm of fists traded punches. Some of Jimmy's mates entered the fight with their own jabs. Splattered claret shone amongst all the whiteness of the shirts. Most of the spectators wouldn't know who had started it all. To Jordy's credit, he held his own, what with dodging four pairs of knuckles and Alana yanking on his now buttonless floral shirt like she was trying to pull him from quicksand. When she went in closer to grab his arm a rogue fist missed its target and she was king hit between the eyes, knocked out cold.

Witi jerked the amplifier cable from his guitar and leapt from the stage. He only swung the old man's guitar once that night but when it hit the back of Jimmy's shoulders it was enough to munt it completely. Jimmy's head hit the polished floor with a sickening noise that seemed to resonate more than any chord Witi had strummed that night. Or killer riff. Witi was left standing with the neck of the guitar in one hand, staring at:

Jordy like he'd survived a close-out at ten-foot Pipeline,

across at Alana who was starting to move,

and the look of horror as the first of the adults, led by the principal, entered the scene. His heart pumped faster than the auto beat still merrily playing in the background.

Let me tell you about wairua, pal.

Your mother took me to her whānau's home on the coast.

She hadn't been back since she was a teenager.

Life had got the better of her, eh. There's always time to get back

but they'd heard she was pregnant.

And head of the family, her dad Koro, had sent one of the nephews
around to tell her

to come home.

We were greeted at the gate by singing, beautiful singing.

Like birds calling us in.

And your mother replied

clearing the spirits between us.

Never heard her sing before, pal, but let's just say I coulda used her in
the band.

Someone to stay on the bus with.

She shared a hongi with her uncles and then the aunties, and I did
the same like, like they thought I was family too.

Shared my breath with them, closest I'd been to any stranger in a long time.

And something inside me sparked.

She stood face to face with Koro for a bit then hugged him for ages.

Afterwards the aunties gushed and some cried in happiness at your mum's stomach.

And there was a big meal that night.

Where Koro watched me eat by myself in the corner of the room.

The next day I sat on the beach and had a staring competition with the sea.

While your mother spoke with Koro up in the whare.

Afterwards they came down to the beach and told me we'd be staying here for a while.

But let me tell you about wairua, pal.

Yeah, soon.

PART II

TOGETHER

Witi had only heard of three others being suspended before:

Kyle had hung out at home and binged on his PlayStation without distraction.

Braden had headed up north to hang out with a sibling at university. He'd come back with a fake ID to prove it.

Ally had spent her time in the city each day hanging out at McDonald's to use the free Wi-Fi to Snapchat mates stuck in college.

It all sounded pretty sweet really.

On the first morning, while Witi was still eating his breakfast, his mum buttoned up her overcoat at the front door and made a comment about the heavy rain warning for later in the day. He could tell she was dark on him by the way she fumbled firmly with her domes.

I'm not sorry for what I did, Mum – he deserved it. But I am for what I've done to you.

Her shoulders levelled again and she allowed a soft smile. She picked the car keys off the hook, told him to do the dishes, then closed the door behind her.

Witi didn't bother doing the dishes straight away. He sat slumped on the edge of his bed and stared at the mess of the guitar's splintered wood and flaccid nylon. The scorn from his peers, the disappointment from the teachers, the disbelief in his mum's face, heck, even the week-long suspension handed down to him, Jordy and Alana from a fired-up principal who'd called a special Board of Trustees meeting the next day – it all meant nothing compared to the guilt that sat like boiling acid in his stomach. People forgive. They tend to get over things. Even if Witi could get the old man's axe fixed, his wairua, the intrinsic energy Mum had referred to, would've well and truly left it in that one violent moment. A week of staring at it in the corner of his room was a punishment he deserved.

He felt a hand on his shoulder. When he turned to look, though, there was nothing but the arrival of the easterly wind on his curtain and a fantail flitting from side to side on the windowsill. He slid off the bed and headed towards the kitchen – suddenly doing the dishes seemed like a good distraction.

He ran the water, oozed the concentrate in and watched the bubbles multiply. He started sliding stuff in and when the sink was chocka he went to turn the tap off. It came off in his hand and water rushed into the sink. He scrambled for the plug but the hot water scalded his hand. Water started heading over the bench and onto the floor. He fumbled with the tap but couldn't make the pieces fit. He grabbed a fish slice, wooden spoon, meat knife – anything long enough to get to the plug. But that plug wasn't budging. The water was pooling around his feet.

Bloody bastard! he yelled. Gimme a break!

And in that moment the water in the sink, the cutlery, plates and glasses, the bubbles, all of it rose up. Levitating right there in front of his eyes, as if he was looking at some sort of goldfish bowl full of crockery. He squinted away, like it was all gonna come tumbling down, but the less he moved, the less it did too. Below it, the tap slowed to a trickle and then completely stopped.

What the ...

He slid his eyes up and saw that the watery mess in the air moved with just a twitch of his fingers.

What the ...

His mobile shrilled and broke his concentration. Everything dropped back into the sink. There was water, bubbles and mess everywhere. How the heck was he gonna clean that up without his mum asking questions? He was panicking. That was all he wanted to think about – dealing with a mess was rational and everyday. This hallucination stuff was getting out of hand.

Just a weird happening, probably with some logical explanation.

Yeah, nothin' to see here. Gonna deal with it myself. Doc Herbert would be proud.

His phone signalled again. He dried his hands and checked it.

R U OM?

Alana texting.

NO @ SKOOL HAHA

Damn good timing, he thought. Dunno how long I should've been left in this kitchen by myself.

WONT MND ME GOIN THRU YA MAIL THEN

He got to where he could see the front gate. Alana was standing like a criminal caught out in the open; a car went past and she crouched into the shadows of their silver pear tree.

Barrelled.

She emerged with a bunch of envelopes and flyers in one hand and waved faintly with the other. Even from this distance Witi could make out the bruising still on her forehead. She looked at her phone and Witi's chirped again:

IS IT SAFE 2 ENTA?

He pushed the window up. You any good at doing dishes? he called.

Witi still felt weirded out about the whole sink thing, but even with water all over the floor, Alana didn't notice; she looked like she was carrying her own little episode. Turned out Alana's parents were at a special packhouse meeting with all employees. It wasn't looking good. Word was the overseas owners had been stung with all the carry-on with financial greed in America or wherever, and they were announcing job losses today.

A perfect storm, some banker dude had called it, enough to cause a giant world depression. Depression in the air. Like a low, Witi guessed.

Epic swells generated from them lows.

He bet those bills in the envelopes Alana dropped on the table were more evidence of it.

As far as he and Alana were concerned, whatever shit was going on in the adult world meant they could hang out without classes or teachers *or* parents.

Sweet, he said.

Yeah, she said.

So they hung out.

Together.

Just hanging, mucking about, talking shit.

Witi made cheese and Marmite sandwiches.

And they streamed music, their soundtrack, and sat on either end of his bed.

She flicked through old surfing mags. He flicked through his dad's old song-writing book.

Their feet touched somewhere in the middle. She didn't move hers, so he didn't either.

Had he heard from Jordy?

Nah, not since he told the principal his son was a *spineless wanker* as he was escorted from the college gymnasium.

Probably shipped off to another college, huh? Alana said.

Too bad, Witi said, He kinda grew on me.

Definitely something about him, she agreed. By the way, you hear the water mains in the gym burst that night? Water everywhere again, just like the other day. If those dickheads had been a few minutes later the teachers would've called the dance off anyway.

But then we wouldn't be here, hanging out, he said.

Alana held up a picture of perfect six-foot Fiji, an empty wave except for the lone coconut tree. Turquoise shimmering off the page.

Imagine if we were *here*, right now, she said. God, what'd you give?

Right there, with her? Everything, probably.

A train sped past and the room rattled.

She turned the page and bit into her sandwich.

Heh, rhetorical. Good one, babe.

Together.

Alana stood on the other side of the room, picked up the guitar but wasn't sure where to hold it. And in that moment Witi had a vision of his dad standing there holding a newborn baby wrapped up in a blanket, his fine muso fingers that could stretch to an F sharp minor eleven with ease now fumbling over which part of the baby he was meant to grasp. He settled for clamping it to his chest and ran through the wall. Witi wiped his eyes. Gathered his mind. Wished for normality when he opened them again.

When he looked, Alana was dragging the instrument behind her. She sat back on the bed.

You could fix it.

Hammer and a few nails should do it.

I'm serious.

I heard the doctor got a jar of splinters out of Jimmy's back. I don't think so.

She picked it back up and laid it across her lap. You could ...

Look at it, babe – it died a noble death.

Alana was trying to work her hand into the opening.

You ever looked at it yourself? she asked. There's something inside. Her patience ran out and she yanked at the wood. The sound threw him back to the haunting moment of impact. She held a shard of guitar in her hands like she was reading it.

What's this doin' in there?

She handed it to him and he looked at the old piece of grey masking tape with the numbers written in bold marker:

8003008

Mean anything to you?

He shook his head. Could be anything.

Like a serial number?

Yeah, maybe.

A birth date? Some date?

He stared at the numbers, familiar numbers. Could be just a coincidence.

Witi?

He ran his fingers over the lines, familiar lines. Familiar curves and stops.

You listening?

He flicked through the pages of the song-writing book.

See how Dad used to write his numbers? They're the same.

Alana studied them and soon nodded. He took the piece back off her and tapped it on an open palm.

Yeah, she said. She smiled and punched him on the side of the arm. You know what this means, don't ya? she said. Why did he put this *in there?*

So let me tell you about wairua, pal.

Koro said mine had been smothered.

Knew it the moment I washed up at the gate, he reckoned

Like a piece of driftwood with ocean in my eyes.

He'd seen that look once before, but didn't say where.

Just that that person never fulfilled their destiny

But it was important I did.

For you, pal.

The next morning before dawn he entered the whare and used his foot to shake me awake.

I didn't like this new hospitality, but he was staunch on it. He was thickset, shorter than me, and when I looked up at him his dreadlocks dangled down like snakes in my face.

I followed him in the darkness down to the beach and when he began wading into the ocean

I stopped in the sand

Sweet, nah.

A wound has to be cleansed before it can heal! he yelled back.

The glow on the horizon was growing bigger and rounder like

like your mother's belly each day.

And I took my first step back into the ocean.

The next ripple ran up my shins and sent sparks through my body.

I joined Koro in waist-deep water and in silence we witnessed the sun break free as waves crashed against us.

This energy has travelled far to greet you today, he said. We know through guys in lab coats with big telescopes how far it's travelled, how long it's taken to reach our skin, how much energy it has. Hell, even how to harness it for our own energy. We think we know everything about anything. We don't know shit. Nature's one big unknown. He cupped his hands in the salt water and washed it against his face. The last drips clung to his beard.

It's never been something to explore and exploit. Nothing could be more dangerous.

I stared at the ocean and it stared back.

The next morning before dawn he entered the whare and shook me again.

Sweet, nah.

But he was staunch on it and nudged me harder with his foot.

You won't get better on leftovers, he said. Get up.

Just go, your mother whispered before rolling over.

We stood in waist-deep water.

We are nature's children, its worshippers. Our ancestors knew this and it was taught through generations as kaitiakitanga, he said.

The sun's energy reached across the ocean and touched us.

We're the first people in the world today to feel this, he said. How does that make you feel?

The next morning before dawn he entered the whare and shook me.

But I'd been awake for a while, listening to the explosions and feeling the whare vibrate.

It's hard to sleep when your name's being called.

Yeah, pal, I hadn't heard that voice in ages.

Outside the whare were four men holding surfboards.

Like warriors in boardies.

The swell arrived overnight, Koro said. Best we greet it, eh, boys?

He reached under the whare and pulled out an old green single fin.

This one's yours, he said, and handed it to me.

I ran my hand down the thick rails and felt the dings and exposed shards of fibreglass.

He found a mal for himself and motioned the others to lead the way.

But I didn't follow.

I felt the end of his longboard poke me in the back.

Don't act like a dummy, he said. I know that look in your eyes. Seen it before, eh.

He marched me down to the beach.

The others had leg-ropes.

Not me.

The others had boards they were used to.

Not me.

I reckon I had the first surfboard ever made.

The perfect board to hongi the ocean with, Koro shouted.

And the others laughed and waded out towards the sound of cracking water.

While ripples ran up my shins.

I walked through the water, guiding the board beside me with the tips of my fingers.

The others had disappeared behind the breaking waves.

I mounted the green surface and began paddling.

And something inside me sparked.

I pierced through the first breaking wave and heard the ocean whisper my name
in the hiss and hum.

And my body absorbed something it hadn't felt in, well ...

I'd forgotten what that felt like, eh, pal.

I paddled past the first guy like he was drifting backwards.

Then duck-dived another wave.

Stalling amongst the hiss and hum.

Caught up to another two and made it under the first proper set wave as the lip came crashing over me

in the hum and hiss again like

like a baby in a womb

on his birthday.

I looked back and the two were left in the white water scrambling for their boards.

The water created a path of ripples all the way out the back, for me.

And I heard words telling me the way

to where Koro and the final surfer sat silhouetted against the new day.

I glided next to them and I straddled my board amongst the large groundswell.

You made it, bro, the surfer said, Rest of us didn't think you could surf.

Nah, sweet.

And Koro smiled.

First wave's mine, the surfer said and began paddling out to meet a new set.

He turned his board back towards land and paddled hard to catch the mass of water.

He flicked to his feet and bottom-turned back into the wave as its lip began covering him

deep in the barrel.

But not as deep as I was, crouched behind him

in the cavity of eternal energy.

He never knew I was there, but I'd been there

before he even knew a set was coming.

He came out of the tube and raised his hands in triumph, celebrating his victory

and I smacked his butt as I manoeuvred past him on my green single fin.

On my birthday.

I CAN'T REACH HIM

Alana was convinced there was some meaning hidden in the numbers.

If his dad had wanted to remember a date he would've written it in a calendar. And if it was a birthday then he only had Witi's and Witi's mum's to remember. So why were the numbers tucked inside something that was so important to him? Alana's fascination persisted. Witi started playing along to humour her, but soon even he was starting to think:

What would he want kept secret?

Even from Mum.

What did he want remembered?

That no one else could remind him about.

See? Alana said. Your dad was way too interesting for this to be nothing.

Witi wanted to show his mum. But he didn't. She had enough to worry about at the moment, and unless these numbers magically brought his dad back, they probably wouldn't spark her day.

He thought about the cops, specifically the detective who'd done his best to find him. He reminded Witi of a teacher, very matter-of-fact. When he told Witi's mum the leads were exhausted and he couldn't do any more he struggled to keep eye contact. Witi had heard that he ran the cop shop in Central now. They kept his contact details in a drawer by the phone. He was ten when the detective wrote them down, tearing off the notepaper and handing it to his mum; back then Witi saw it as a hotline to help. That piece of paper used to float on top of everything in that drawer, but over the years it'd sunk beneath stuff like rates receipts and a Ging and Sing's take-away menu. The detective still sent them a Christmas card each year with the same sincere condolences and half-promises that kept a faint pulse going for the following year.

Yeah, nah.

That detective means well, his mum said, but your father is very good at hiding himself where no one can find him.

He can sit where you are and I can't reach him. I'll call his name but he disappears, like the rest of us aren't there. Sometimes for a moment, other times for days. And comes back when he's good and ready. Then again, maybe he's hiding us, has put us in this other world where he can't be bothered by us? Can write silly songs and play that stupid guitar and surf those damn boards to his heart's content.

Sorry, son, got carried away. Didn't mean it. Your father's got a beautiful mind.

Yeah, she still talked of him in the present tense.

For the next couple of days the numbers appeared wherever Witi looked – an 800 on TV, a 300 across the radio, an 8 on the tide charts, then on the microwave, on his watch, on his phone, in the paper, on the muesli box, on his bedside clock, on the surf wax packet, other people's Insta stories – same fuckin' numbers everywhere.

Just never in the same order.

One day to go on the suspension and Witi's mum got a morality kick. Decided she was gonna teach Witi a lesson, or maybe provide him with an opportunity to think about things.

I want you to clean the shed, she told him over breakfast. It's time we started to move on.

He protested. Whadabout Dad?

If he was going to come back every time someone messed around with his stuff he would've been here when his guitar was smashed, she said. The only ones enjoying his things out there are the bugs and mice. Seems a shame, don't you reckon? You tidy it up and I'll bring some boxes home from work. Be nice to have a place to park the car for once.

Yeah, nah, he's got a heap of crap in there.

She smiled and held her hand on her heart. I'm not asking you to tidy the space you have for your dad in here, son, just a shed with some old gear in it. That's all.

It took Witi a while to wrench the main door open but eventually it opened in a roar of metal. He felt the shed inhale for the first time in many years. It looked way smaller with this much light, although it was probably because he was heaps shorter the last time he stood right here. Two nesting birds suddenly made a break for the open space; they blurred past either side of his head and he was left on his backside in the driveway.

Every broom sweep stirred up a dust storm.

Every object was secured by cobwebs.

He pulled his phone from his pocket and texted Alana.

FREE AKCESS TO DADS STUFF

She turned up shortly after and offered to help.

Arranging things: this over here, that over there. Witi got window-cleaning product and a cheese and Marmite sandwich each and when they sat down to eat Alana joked how they could fit half of his mum's car in there now.

His girlfriend but not his girlfriend.

Nesting.

Later, he was carefully filing some of his old man's surfboards into the rafters when Alana called him over to a cupboard she'd been rummaging in.

Check this out. She held up a small brass box.

Nothing too out of the ordinary in this place, except that it was locked. She shook it to dull thuds. There were no markings on the outside besides their fingerprints in the dust. Witi tried to lever it with a screwdriver, but the seal was too tight. He banged the top of the screwdriver with a hammer, but it barely made a mark. Alana had disappeared so he stuck the box in a vice and prepared to give it everything. Alana returned and calmly freed the box from the grip and took it outside.

Hey!

Males, she scoffed.

Witi tossed the hacksaw onto the workbench. I had it, he said.

She sat cross-legged on the concrete and with a cloth began wiping the box clean. A thin plaque appeared. With her fingers she gently slid it open, exposing a combination lock mechanism.

Bingo, she said.

Pfft, gonna pick it, are ya?

She gave him the piece of guitar with the numbers on it. Read these out, she said.

As he did, her thumb clicked through the combination, and on the final number the lid opened without a satisfactory sound.

After the first surf session your mother said she saw something different in me.

A glow

a fizz in the eyes

a new spring in my footprints left in the sand.

She couldn't explain it, eh.

Koro said that's 'cos you can't explain infinity

but he'd try to

soon.

The next morning before dawn I was already waiting for them outside.

Even pulled the green single fin out from under the whare and waxed it.

But they never came.

Nah, it's Sunday, Koro told me over breakfast. That's sleep-in day.

At low tide we piled onto the back of an old blue Land Rover truck and drove a few kilometres down the beach to where the sand became solid reef.

The same men I surfed with the day before started getting their dive gear ready

and one handed me a set of goggles and snorkel and a screwdriver.

Got kaimoana before? he asked.

Yeah, nah, and I started using the flathead to scratch a number in the paint of the tray at the back of the truck.

We went out onto the edge of the reef and the others became submerged amongst the kelp and rocky ledges.

I turned back to the beach and in the distance saw your mother and a couple of aunties collecting seaweed along the foreshore.

Truth was, pal, they all looked pregnant from that distance.

I guessed it was the one waving back to me

with eyes like

circles of paua shell.

I left the flippers and snorkel, dive belt and gloves and flathead screwdriver on the reef.

I put on the goggles and looped the dive bag around my wrist.

I reckoned I could hold my breath forever, but I'd never tried.

I stepped into the water and went deeper until I sunk under the surface into the

hiss and hum.

Bath tub, sink, bird fountain, holy water, whatever.

There were plenty of paua to keep me busy.

They jumped from their possies into my palm.

And crays would come out from under the ledges to see who this new type of fish was and I'd point into the open bag and they'd happily walk in.

Threw some kina in there too, for good measure.

One of the others in the group must've seen me go under and not come up.

'Cos suddenly there was all this commotion around me and a big hand clasped my arm and hauled me to the surface.

You alive, bro? someone said.

I held my bag up, higher than my smile.

Fish inna water, eh.

Later we prepared the kaimoana on the veranda and listened to Bob Marley.

I learnt to bang the flesh of the paua on a rock then use my thumb to scoop it out.

I watched the guys use a knife to slice the kina in half and drink its flesh like a glass of water.

I observed the aunties hanging the seaweed out in the sun to dry and was given stuff prepared earlier to snack on while we put the crays in big pots of boiling water and minced the paua flesh.

And drank beer from crates.

Except me, of course.

Your mother said I had enough toxins in my body to last me three lifetimes.

A beautiful mind, eh.

Damn good reggae.

Biggest feed ever that night, pal.

I sat in-between Koro and your mother.

Hadn't laughed like that for ...

Since I'd ...

Mighta been ...

Nah, couldn't remember the last time.

Whole other lifetime ago, eh.

They prepared a big fire under the stars,

a black ocean of your mother's eyes

and someone pulled a guitar out and I thought

sweet, nah

but for the next three hours everyone else played it

'cept me.

Same four-beat strum used in a medley of classics.

Fuelled on kaimoana and crate beer.

I'd been around the world and I'd never heard singing like it, pal.

They never knew who I was, who I'd been.

Felt like the only one in the crowd.

Someone passed it to Koro

and said, Play us 'Ten Guitars' again.

But he stood and handed it to me.

You play us something, he said.

And the others agreed.

I looked to your mother and she winked

like a star in the night sky.

So I did

A simple four-beat strum they'd know the words to

and something inside me ignited.

NOT HOW I REMEMBERED

Witi hadn't seen that black book with the leather cover and gold lining for so long he must've removed it from his memories of the old man. Or maybe Dr Herbert helped him do it. As a kid it represented being boring. Dad's diary. But now it was all surging back to Witi: he'd battled against it for his dad's attention. It had given him a bad vibe because his dad never wrote in the open, like in front of Witi and his mum or at the kitchen table. Only secretively.

In the backyard sitting against the fence.

On the sand after a surf.

In his artefact room.

In a tree, once.

Yeah, nah.

He'd go off, try to be private so he could write, but Witi would find him every time.

Yet here it was in a brass box, kept under lock and dust. Minded by the bugs and mice crap.

Alana lifted it out and flicked through the pages, revealing fine handwriting and sporadic sketches. She slammed it shut.

I shouldn't be looking at this, she said. It's private. And she handed it up to Witi.

Maybe she expected Witi to jump into it and read it out aloud.

But he felt its heavy weight in his hand and rubbed the soft leather with one thumb and teased the bottom corner of the cover with the other. He stared at it until the brown and gold blurred with tears.

You okay? Alana asked.

They'd finally found him again.

Witi hardly slept that night.

And he didn't show for breakfast either.

He hadn't finished reading it.

When his mum knocked on his bedroom door and asked if he was okay he told her he was sweet, just a little knackered from the work the day before and he'd be up soon. When he heard her footsteps leave he pulled the diary out from under his pillow and continued reading. If she knew what was written in there ... The mum he knew would never understand. Hell, he didn't understand, but he felt he wanted to, needed to. He didn't know why, but the stuff in the diary wasn't normal. It wasn't all decipherable, and when it was, it was raw and prosy. Like he remembered his dad. Stop, start, often incoherent. But he heard his voice as he read it silently and if he *was* reading it right, it offered a new direction.

Alana turned up at their house. Sounded like she bumped into his mum at the front door as she was leaving for work. A few words, then Alana burst into his bedroom.

Whoah, she said, pausing, you look like crap. I was gonna ring, but nah. Anyway, *what did it say*?

Witi wasn't sure how much to tell her, what was important, what wasn't. So he started with some of the interesting stuff, but the more questions she asked the more the other stuff came out naturally.

Geez, this is not how I remember him.

You were just a kid. Look at us now, eighteen and we still don't have a clue.

The one thing they could understand was the map at the back. By lunch-time that had become their focus. His dad had traced a coastal map and made marks and drawings, some of them familiar from the stuff in the spare room. But most importantly they recognised it as the place they'd been to a few days earlier, the piece of coastline his dad said held so much spiritual connection to Witi and his mum.

Alana tried to help work out some of the cryptic things, but by mid-morning she'd resorted to pencil and paper and making some notes. Afterwards, she put the end of the pencil in her mouth and looked pleased with herself. This is what we're working with, she said:

What if…

He was writing a novel and these were his notes? (Alana's idea).

He was taking drugs? (Alana's idea).

He was having psychiatric issues and this was his therapy? (Alana's idea).

This was therapy that eventually turned into a metaphor for something else? (Alana's idea).

What if, Alana, he's still out there somewhere? *What if* it's actually all true?

Witi, she said, showing him her dimples, I reckon you need some sleep.

She made him lie down on his bed. He felt her get comfortable against him with the diary and he closed his eyes.

But yeah, what if? he whispered.

Your wairua never leaves you forever, pal.

Despite what you might think.

It just gets lost from time to time.

Koro and I went for a surf.

We sat on our surfboards a long way past the breaking waves

but not so far that I couldn't look back and see your mother lounging on the beach with her t-shirt pulled up.

Her giant brown tummy in the sun and the offshore breeze –

must've felt nice in there, eh, pal?

Mauri is the life force behind all things in this world, Koro told me.

Everything has it, even this wave approaching us.

He pointed at the sun directly above.

It starts up there, millions of miles away.

Its energy travels to Earth each day.

Sometimes it'll help form a high in the weather and things will be nice for a while.

Other times it'll form a low,
a dense circle of energy on the map,
a violent storm that'll transform the surface of the ocean
and make it thrash and surge like a wahine giving birth.

Think about that, eh.

This wave is the love child of the sun and the ocean.

It's the same energy, reincarnated.

Then he looked at me, pal, his smile forming thick lines of swell in the
skin outside his eyes.

But it doesn't stop there, he continued, no.
Us surfers catch it.

Absorb its mauri.

Take it back to land with us
to share with family and friends
and fuel our wairua.

We're the lucky ones, eh.

To get such a direct line to the big guy.

For the next two months he taught me how
everything, right down to the rock in his hand, has a story and a
whakapapa that can be traced
and we don't live in the world we think we do,
the one that's shown on the six o'clock news.

There's another dimension called Te Kore beyond our own reality that houses an eternal source of mauri, the beginning of all things.

Kinda like heaven without the angels and shiny white gates, I guess.

He told me about a recurring dream he'd had of someone controlling
the door to Te Kore,
someone with ocean in their eyes
who could even step in and out of the door,
like a resurrection.

But like everything in this world, Man was learning about it. Wanting
to explore and exploit it with science and machines. Such terrible
consequences, he assured me.

And he taught me how all things give off a vibration:

tiny sound waves in the air

coming from you and me

the ocean and the plants

the wind and running water.

Even music, pal. I'd never thought about that before, eh?

Good vibrations, he told me.

Like your ancestors used to say? I asked.

Nah, he said. The Beach Boys.

A BIG FARKIN' NOR'EAST SWELL

Jordy phoned Witi real late that night, waking him up.

Jordy had been grounded over the last few days too and in the process he'd made an exciting discovery amongst his own dad's stuff.

Unfarkinbelievable, came his voice down the line. He didn't wait for Witi to respond, instead went full salesman on him:

Perfect reef formation.

Only a few hours' drive from here.

Secluded, no one likely for miles.

Would have to drive so far and then hike in to get to it.

Has all the makings of another Uluwatu, or reverse Bells Beach.

A goofy-footer's utopia.

He had the maps to prove it.

Just needs a westerly wind

and a big farkin' nor'east swell.

Bigger the better, eh. Wouldn't work on anything else.

Like the one brewing. The one all over the news at the moment.

He finally paused. You in? he asked.

Witi looked at the clock on his phone. 12:15am. If this wasn't a dream it was surely a stitch-up.

He yawned. Yeah, sure.

Great. I'll come round when I can and we'll plan it. Gonna be your chance to shine, brother.

Unfarkinbelievable, he repeated, and hung up.

Witi dropped his phone into the darkness and went back to sleep.

Once the dreams started, pal, they didn't stop.

The first one came with such force I woke sitting up in bed

gasping like I'd been starved of breath or

I was taking my very first.

And your mother said I was too hot to touch.

So she made me go and stand outside in the rain.

In the dark I heard the sea

and knew something was coming.

The second dream came a few days later, the third two nights after that. Soon I lost track.

It was like the dream was just waiting for me to put my head on the pillow.

So it could sit me back up again. All with the same sudden intensity.

Your mother kept a bucket of water and a cloth next to her.

She'd wipe me down and sing to me in a whisper.

Coulda used her in the band if I'd known.

One morning she spoke to Koro about my recurring dreams.

She was worried about me again.

And he rubbed his whiskers and nodded.

He said my wairua was leaving me during the night and coming back with visions, but that's all he could say.

It got tough, pal.

I'd stay awake at night.

Too scared to sleep.

But Koro said I'd have to embrace the dreams. It was my wairua speaking to me.

So I closed my eyes

Next thing I know I'm sitting up again in the dark and your mother is reaching for the bucket.

Koro taught me a karakia, a prayer. Said it would help protect me and anyone I said it to. Couldn't speak Māori, but I knew how to sing so pretended it was a song.

I'd sing it to myself at night.

Quietly, in my head.

Sang it to you on your birthday down on the shore.

But the wairua didn't care for prayers after a while.

Something was coming, it was tellin' me.

I tried writing it down.

Drawing pictures.

But the pages stayed blank.

The best I could do was scribble to black out the page.

Something was coming.

An army of lines,
soldiers marching
towards us all.

Circles and ovals
forming and breaking and regenerating.

Cavities of massive energy,
destruction and existence,
scribbles on the page
in my mind.

Both parts

energy

energy.

Something is coming.

WE WERE NEXT

It'd only taken two days for Cyclone Trudy to leave Fiji in a mess of flattened houses, swollen rivers of silt, eroded beaches. A missing persons list, one reporter said, would've had more on it than those left alive in the islands.

There'd been total annihilation.

Aid was being flown in from all corners of the globe.

All except New Zealand.

The planes couldn't get past Trudy and her circles within circles on the map on the TV screen.

We're going to experience unprecedented air pressure of eight hundred as the cyclone builds in intensity, the weather man said.

This meant nothing to Witi and his mum, but they saw the sweat on his face and heard the tremor in his voice through the TV's tiny speakers and knew that whatever it was, it must be serious.

And wind speeds up to three hundred kilometres an hour that will generate swells in excess of eight metres.

Bet he never thought he'd be announcing impending devastation. Thought it'd be all corny weather jokes and one-liners to the anchor man. He never signed up for this, eh.

Right now he was the most important guy in the country.

People had already started evacuating from coastal towns and settlements.

And a state of civil emergency had been declared from Northland to Otago.

Hardware stores had high demand for wood and nails and anything else to protect windows and doors.

There were queues at petrol stations and the shelves in supermarkets were emptied.

Populations of inland towns like Taupo had surged to record numbers.

No one had seen this type of paranoia in eight years since Cyclone...

The TV screen blacked out and Mum rested the remote back on the arm of the couch.

Don't need to see that, she said.

Sounds pretty important, though.

Don't worry, son, just media hyping everything out of proportion. Bad news sells, eh.

They sat in silence, except for his mum's fingers fidgeting.

Witi's mind was full of noise though:

Eight years since, huh?

Heh, eight round years.

Circle upon circle.

Going forever. The infinity symbol.

Or a couple of eyes.

Nah, yeah.

They sat in silence, except for the fidgeting still coming from his mum.

He looked up,

Mum, who was Father O'Reilly?

Your mum was uncomfortable all day, pal.

Complaining about this and that.

She unsettled the rest of the whare 'cos all the aunties were fidgety and pacing and lurking in every room I went into.

They couldn't stop smilin', eh.

And the uncles were keeping a wide berth of the place, like they always had something else to do.

But even they seemed more upbeat than usual.

Felt like everyone had heard the punch line except me.

Koro musta known something was up 'cos late in the afternoon he called me down to the beach.

I haven't got much time, he said.

Didn't know what he meant, eh, so I asked him, straight up.

It's not important, he said. What's important is that you take this.

He handed me a bone carving. I held it in my palm and I could feel the mauri of the carver in its weight. It surged in me like it was embracing me. Like when a parent chose one of the orphans.

The thin woven strands that hung from two small holes felt strong.

You must take this, he continued. Take this and when your son is the right age you must give him a half.

My son?

Do you understand?

But how do you know?

Do you understand?

I nodded.

We heard a yell from the whare. Someone had spilt water every-where.

You were born before dinner-time, pal.

My son.

A BEAUTIFUL MIND

He showed his mum the diary.

He had so many questions he didn't know where to start.

But his mum flicked through the pages and sighed. The way she was holding her head made him want to snatch the diary back from her.

There's something you need to know about your father that I should've told you a long time ago.

She stopped on one page and shook her head and smiled, but not with humour. She was remembering something that hurt. Witi leaned over and saw thick black scribbles. She ran her finger along the strokes.

Such a beautiful mind, she said. God knows I did my best to compete with it. I was determined to help him harness it, control it. But his obsessions and his music were his gatekeepers. I remember towards the end once trying to ask him a question and he replied with a riff from his guitar. He was truly sick. Of course, you wouldn't have known this at your age, son, but this diary gives you an idea of it.

She flicked to the back pages.

He was eventually writing in prose like his life was some ballad, she continued. Back then they didn't try and explain people like your dad. They tried to pigeonhole him as depressed and schizophrenic.

Some said he was autistic. Once upon a time a white padded van would've turned up at the gate to take him away. Not like these days – they're inventing a name for it every week. Could've saved him a dozen times over if he was here now. Then again, she said, makes it sound simple doesn't it?

She tried smiling at Witi but it released tears instead. He hadn't seen her do that in ages. She wiped them.

This diary was the last of it, she said. He was long gone from me by the time this appeared. I used to read it at night when he thought ... well, I couldn't save him by then anyway so it didn't matter what he thought. I think he wanted you to have it, though.

It was locked away, Witi said. It's a fluke I ever found it.

She laughed. Nothing was a fluke with him, son. He wanted you to find it when you did.

She closed it softly and handed it back.

Your dad's life always ran parallel with the rest of us. Father O'Reilly died when your dad was sixteen. I know because I was like you at one stage. The official medical report said it was a heart attack but when I knocked on the doors of some original houses down by the harbour, where those new seaside apartments are now, the few who remembered him painted a picture of a mad Irishman who prayed to a god at the bottom of a liquor bottle.

Father O'Reilly was on a mission with him, Witi said.

Sorry, son, he was just searching for answers, like the rest of us. The only thing he can be credited with is finding your father at the front door when he was baby – highly unlikely that ever happened. Think about it. Oh, he did leave the stack of dusty albums we've got in the shed outside. And of course he identified your father's creative ability early on and set him down a path that nurtured it.

That was a good thing?

Her shoulders rose slowly. Maybe. Without proper mentoring your father's mind was never going to survive the pressure Oval Records put on him. Creative minds are famous for depression and anxiety, drug abuse, all the sad stuff. Especially a beautiful mind like your father's. His was the most creative of the lot. Except maybe for yours, she said and winked.

He reckoned you thought he was a genius?

She looked over at the notebook, like maybe she wanted to read those parts again.

He made a lot of people a lot of money, she said, but it fell through his hands like water. Does that make him a genius? You've seen the pages in that diary, the stories, the symbols, the paranoia. After Oval Records he thought *everyone* was out to get him. So he created a barrier around himself that pretty much housed him, me and you. He loved you so much. But without his connection to music like he remembered, he resorted to creating elaborate stories of his prowess and his destiny and how he had to protect the world from secret groups set on destroying it. Conspiracy theories, crazy stuff like that. It's all in there, she said, pointing at the diary. Son, his mind was so active it ran away from the guy I instantly fell in love way back when we were teenagers. All I had left was the ghost of him wandering around the house in a pair of underpants until one day that disappeared as well.

He was a sick man, son, she said and slid across the couch. She threw an arm behind Witi and suddenly they were one. I won't let you fall to the same fate. You need to start moving on with your life.

NOWHERE ELSE TO GO

The next morning Witi woke to a man's voice outside. It was deep and salty, kinda recognisable, but . . .

but, nah, couldn't be.

Witi pulled the curtain and pressed his face to the glass to see who was at the front door, yet could only make out the back of long grey dreadlocks. His mum was there, her words muffled but antsy. An old blue Land Rover was parked in the driveway.

He was still in the doorway when Witi came around. His mum looked like she was stopping the guy from entering. They were talking over each other, but when he saw Witi standing behind her he went silent. She turned and must've seen the look on Witi's face.

He has your eyes, the man said, but the rest's his dad, eh.

Doesn't mean you can come in, she said, turning back to him. Kaumatua or not.

He's my mokopuna, he said. I have rights.

I'm not your daughter anymore, she said. I made that clear to you at the time when I told you never to come here.

She tried to shut the door.

But he put his foot at its base and it stopped suddenly.

Something's coming, he said, just like last time, but worse. I can't stay on the coast and I've got nowhere else to go.

He looked at Witi again and raised his eyebrows. Witi saw the lines of swell in his skin.

But this man was much older than he'd imagined.

He looked soft and worn down. Full of stories, likely.

Here on their doorstep like a piece of driftwood.

Yet something about him was still alive,

glowing inside.

My grandfather.

Nah, never knew, eh.

Mum, Witi said quietly.

Mum.

Let him in.

Witi offered to let him sleep in his bed and he'd crash on a mattress. His grandfather was dropping his bag off in Witi's room before his mum had a chance to object. By the time he came back Witi had the jug turned on and a loaf of bread and Marmite ready on the bench.

You had breakfast? Witi asked.

Kia ora, lad, he said with a nod. Looks good.

His mum grabbed her coat and slammed the door behind her.

The old man sat down and watched Witi throw a teabag in the mug and pour the water.

Witi looked up at him and grinned.

Didn't know where to start, eh.

Just kept grinning and pouring.

His grandfather was looking around the room, sussing it out or maybe looking for some evidence of his dad's existence.

Your mother never told you about me? he said after a while.

Witi shook his head. Nah, never knew, eh.

How old are you? he asked. Fifteen? Sixteen?

Eighteen.

He grunted and his gaze fell away. Witi slid the drink to him and he mumbled a thank you. He took a sip.

Me and you got some catching up to do then, eh?

Yeah.

You surf?

Yeah.

Play the guitar?

Yeah.

His smile had holes in it where his teeth were missing.

Then we're halfway there already, he said.

They spent the morning around the Formica table. It was weird having someone from his dad's diary sitting opposite him in real life. Specially such a close relative. Sensing Witi's uncertainty, he told him to call him Koro, like everyone else did.

Sorry Mum isn't as stoked to see you, he said.

She was always fiercely independent, your mum. Coast could never keep her, eh. She left us early on as a teenager, promised she'd be back, but, yeah. Liked the bright lights and big city stuff. Shoulda been born a moth. Funny how she fell in love with a pakeha with ocean in his eyes, then, eh?

He hadn't seen Witi since he was born. Told Witi his placenta was buried behind the whare and a totora tree planted above it. He said his mum and dad took him back to this house a week or so later. The last piece of communication he had with his mum was their car skidding away up the gravel road. He still made a point to visit the tree every day since, reckoned it was the strongest on the coast.

The old man seemed to like you, Witi said – from what I read, anyway.

Your dad was special, he said. He had something he had to do, an important act, a destiny to fulfil.

He was a successful musician.

Koro shook his head. Nah, that was just his talent. This other thing was much more than that. Unfortunately his strong creative spirit clouded it, and when I cleared him of that, something else came up I couldn't compete with.

Witi wasn't sure what he was talking about.

Your mother's love for the guy. She never embraced your father's destiny and figured I was going to undo all the good work so she brought him back here to protect him.

Koro nodded his head to the window.

Like this culture can do, he said. It's all fake concrete and blind greed. This was the last place for a guy like your dad to wind up in.

He came from the ocean, eh. Knew that fact from the moment he stood in the whare. I recognise his mauri in you. Bet you miss him.

I got memories, Witi said, but, yeah.

Koro stared at him like he was waiting for more. His eyes bullied Witi's and he had to look away. He felt Koro drawing him in again and he couldn't escape.

Sometimes he's still ... Witi started.

Sometimes he still ...

The other night in the hallway ...

Yes, lad, yes?

Nah, nothing.

He's still here, isn't he? You see him still.

Witi shrugged. In my head, he said. Been there since he left.

Yes, but he's not just in your head.

Dr Herbert said he is.

Koro laughed. What does Dr Herbert know, huh?

He's the best shrink in the valley. Got a framed certificate on his wall and everything.

And you believe him?

Witi screwed his mouth up. Nah, haven't been back for ages. He's a dickhead.

Yeah, thought as much.

Alana came round to the house and told Witi she was moving with her parents to Hamilton next week after her dad got a new job in a freezing works up there. She started crying and Witi held her in his arms and stroked her back. Just like that, their world was changing. Koro walked into the room and when Alana looked up she let out a sharp scream. Witi introduced them.

Kia ora, lass, he said. He pulled her close and went to kiss her cheek. But Alana pushed him back politely and made out she was happy with a handshake.

Don't worry, he's from the coast, Witi said. They're old school out there.

But over the afternoon Alana got to know Koro too:

My girlfriend, but not my girlfriend.

Same waxhead of a dad as me.

My one groupie.

And all that stuff.

Koro gave Witi a wink. He knew she got him.

When she explained why she was leaving for Hamilton, Koro sat back on the chair and rubbed his chin.

You're both victims of greed, he said. Everyone's in search of the dollar. And when they've got it, all anyone thinks about is how to get more. So they sell ya, huh? Sometimes those with plenty of it join up with others the same and try to control everyone else. Even the natural world. He leant in. As well as the world everyone's forgotten.

Alana nodded, but she didn't get him. Buggered if Witi knew either.

There is a clash of tides coming, he continued, between greed and the natural order. We've got one last chance before this false culture takes you both and everyone with it. Something's coming and you're gonna need to be ready. You need to stand up to it, be staunch, like a totora tree.

BLACK

Witi is sitting on his surfboard in a deep valley in a mountain range.

The Southern Alps, or the Andes, maybe the Himalayas.

Dunno where.

The slopes sparkle where moonlight catches them

as the mountains move in rage.

In silence.

Giant lines, one after the other.

Soldiers in formation.

An army.

Marching not on land at all.

But in the ocean.

He rises on a crest and sees land in the distance, a single light

directly in their path.

He yells his warning:

Something is coming!

But the offshore wind blows it back at him.

And he's again in a trough,

in the shadow of the next wave,

still yelling

as the wave folds in half and falls

falls

falls

down on him.

Driving him into the depths.

His board plucked from his hands like a leaf in the wind.

Deeper he goes, his ears stinging.

Blackest colour he's ever seen.

Black scribbles.

Nothing but thick black energy and his screams.

Something is coming.

Witi sat up in bed,

Wet like he'd been submerged.

Gasping like he'd just made it to the surface.

So your wairua speaks to you too, lad.

Best we talk in the morning.

HE TALKS TO THE SEA

Koro wasn't in his bed when Witi woke.

He walked into the kitchen. Koro and his mum were at opposite ends of the table. Koro was bent over, channelling cereal into his mouth with a spoon he held in his fist. His dreadlocks were tied back with a bit of material in Rastafarian colours. Red, green and gold, a spaghetti factory explosion. His mum sat like a mannequin at the other end. Witi saw the emotional drain by the way she was staring at him. She looked as cold as the full mug of tea at her fingertips.

Witi prepared his own cereal and sat between them with a spoon poised.

Koro wiped his mouth with the back of his hand.

Morena, lad. Good sleep? He smiled, showing Weet-Bix in the gaps.

His mum said she had to get to work. She walked round and kissed Witi's forehead.

I had my reasons for not telling you, she whispered. We'll talk tonight, okay?

Witi waited for her to leave the house, the property. The car engine finally revved.

Where's my old man? he asked Koro.

Soon, lad.

Koro wanted a tour of the house. So Witi showed him the backyard boxed in by a railway track and neighbours, the shed clean enough for a car to be parked. Here Koro took a particular liking to the green single fin amongst the other surfboards. He ran his fingers in the heel dents in the wax.

I know this board, he said. Your dad made this thing dance.

But Witi got the feeling Koro wanted more. He was looking for something else, some clue, sign or proof, something other than this everyday stuff.

What's on the end of that necklace of yours? he asked. Can I see?

Sure. Witi pulled it out. It's just something ...

Koro looked excited. Your dad gave it to you. Yes?

How'd ya know?

I gave it to him. On the day of your birth, lad.

So you know what it means?

Oh, yes, lad. We can talk about it.

Now?

Soon, lad, soon.

When Witi showed him the special room inside he became even more animated, like he'd hit the jackpot. He began flicking through the piles of paper, scrapbooks, the maps, the scribbles – all of it like he was reading a language no one except him understood. And Witi started to worry that this was what his mum was protecting him from. That he'd started something he couldn't take back.

You hungry? I'll put the jug on ...

That's just old newspaper, nuthin' interesting ...

Dunno why Dad saved that, heh – look at it. Junk.

C'mon, I'll get that jug on, eh?

Witi was struggling to move him on. He needed to speak with his mum, to figure stuff out.

His time *did* come, Koro said, excited.

With what?

He looked at Witi like he should know. Protecting us, lad.

The words caused a ring in Witi's ears.

Koro chuckled. Son of a bitch, he said.

There were thumps at the front door, with barely a pause between each set.

It was Jordy, holding a large brown cardboard folder.

Heard you'd moved, Witi said.

First time I've ever come back. He went inside, brushing past Witi.

Koro had followed Witi so he introduced Jordy to him.

Fark me, ya related to Bob Marley too?

But Koro simply flicked his head and eyebrows at Jordy and disappeared back up the hallway. Witi guessed he couldn't do much about Koro's snooping anymore so he let him go. Jordy was all agitated anyway, and apart from the confused look and the silent thumb in

Koro's direction, he didn't seem interested in him. Instead he started spreading bits of paper out on the table. Like this house needed more of that sort of stuff.

How you been doin' your time? Witi asked.

Old man skint me of anything cool and put me under house arrest, Jordy said.

Tough love, huh?

I'm not the one with a dreadlocked prison warden wanderin' the house. Jordy pointed to the paper. Check it out. I got to rummaging through my ol' man's stuff, and I found these nuggets. Dad might be a genius but he's a disorganised one.

Jordy had it planned. The bits of paper showed maps, all to scale, done on a computer – real professional looking. Numbers and letters like a language for geeks. He made the same pitch he did over the phone. But this time he showed Witi:

the coast east of there.

The perfect reef formation.

And told him:

We'd have to drive to here, then hike to there.

All the makings of Uluwatu, or a reverse Bells Beach.

Dunno, bro, Witi said.

You got a reputation to build, Jordy said. You think knocking out the rugby captain is your calling? They'll make a statue of you in that shithouse college of yours after this ...

He posed like a robot.

You're nuts.

Farkin' oath I am. I'm makin' history and you're comin' with me. It's a goofy-footer's wet dream.

Gimme a look at those, Koro said from behind them.

He pushed between them and started examining the maps. Jordy swallowed loudly and soon got fidgety. Koro looked at some sheets extra times, and the more he did the more he nodded.

See, Jordy said, see? Your pop gets it.

Koro turned to him. Jordy was a big guy, but Koro looked like he could've been a strainer post once upon a time.

What's your whakapapa, lad?

Eh? Jordy looked around at Witi. Eh?

Where you from? Region? Heritage? What's your mountain? What's your river? What waka did you arrive in?

Fark, dunno any of that. Arrived on a Qantas flight if that helps. Dunno its number, though.

He's Australian, Witi said. It was kinda funny.

Thought as much, Koro said. Then let me tell you about your little discovery here.

He told Jordy that Witi's marae – where Koro and others from their whānau lived – was situated not far from this point on the map. Their ancestors arrived in the area hundreds of years ago and while many had scattered over time, Witi's roots were in this piece of coastline and could be easily traced, from the river to the canoe. Witi was hearing this for the first time, but Koro made out this was all old news to him and Koro was only telling Jordy for Witi's sake. And Witi had never felt such a strong connection to anything before.

I know about this wave you're talking about, he added. You're right, it's not the sort of place to decide on the morning you're goin' to it. Unless – and he looked at Witi – you have good reason to.

You seen it? Jordy asked.

Yeah, I seen it. He lifted his shirt to reveal disfigured skin down his side. And surfed it.

Nup, no way, Jordy said smiling. He looked at Witi. I'm calling BS on your pop.

Witi looked at Koro and saw the same steely glare Jordy could see. Koro kept it there for good effect.

Mind you, Koro continued, that was only double overhead. It was just playin' with me. Coulda killed me a dozen times over.

Jordy still wasn't sure what to make of him. Was it perfect, though? he finally asked.

You know those pictures you see in the mags, Koro said, of Hawaii and Indo? Got nothin' on it, eh, not even close. Perfection, like God himself was a surfer.

That evidently sealed the deal for Jordy. He made a smug sound. *Knew* it, he said. And the best bit – with my mate Witi here, we're technically not even trespassing.

Jordy had to get back – before it was noticed he'd broken out – so he ordered an Uber and was gone.

Koro was curious to see what the central city looked like these days, considering he hadn't been there for over twenty years, so he and Witi walked to the train station and caught a ride in. Witi took Koro to the street corner where he and his dad use to busk. They sat and ate ice-creams and watched the people walking past. They did this in silence for the most part; Koro's breathing was like drawn-out sighs. Like he was in a state of constant disappointment with what he was seeing.

What do you make of Jordy? Witi asked.

Gritty fullah, eh?

Heh, yeah.

When Koro got to the end of the cone he threw it to the birds at their feet.

We'll need to get you back if you're heading out with him.

He's dreamin', Witi said. Not even sure half his stories are right.

Test him then. Call his bluff.

You evacuated the coast and you're telling me to head out?

The wave doesn't break on anything smaller.

Geez, no wonder Mum was dark about you.

Witi had a sudden urge to retract that comment. Would've if he had a chance. But Koro just buried his hands in his pockets and slouched lower in the seat. His head followed three pedestrians marching in formation and speaking on their phones.

The day I surfed it I wasn't by myself, lad, he said. Your father was there too.

Dad?

Shoulda seen 'im. He was taking only the biggest set waves.

And suddenly Koro got up and stood in the middle of the foot-path.

From where I was sitting, lad, he was just a stick figure in the distance. The waves did their best to swallow him, but each time he disappeared he'd pop out in a cannon blast of sea spray, fingers extended above his head like he was writing the whole thing with his hands. Like an artist, a sculptor, a musician conducting.

Koro almost took a lady out with his arm as he shaped the curves of the barrel.

Did he get smashed on the reef too?

Nah, lad, he talks to the sea. Waves respect him.

He looked at Witi like he was waiting for something from him. Buggered if Witi knew what, though, so he looked away. It was weird-ing him out.

You find yourself looking at water? Koro asked. Wondering how it moves like that?

Eh?

Goes naturally down a sink hole in clockwise, but it can go the other way if you want it to? Ever seen that?

I don't know what ...

Asked yourself why the ocean mothers *you*? You hear them voices too, don't ya?

Witi wiped his eyes, trying to clear away whatever the hell his grandfather was referring to.

Koro picked at the silver stubble on his chin. Yeah, you've got that same look your dad gave me all those years ago. Reckon you know *exactly* what I'm talking about.

Bet Mum would've had kittens, Witi said, to bring the subject back. You two taking off like that.

He smiled – like he was satisfied he'd got what he was looking for – and sat back next to Witi.

Not quite, he said. She'd just had you the day before. Told your mum we were off looking at an old pa site and we'd be back at dinnertime. Can you believe it? He started laughing. A brand-new father and grandfather doin' a runner on her to go surfing! He hooted with such intensity he broke into a coughing frenzy. No one walking past seemed interested.

You risked the relationship you had with her for a surf?

Not just a surf, lad. A practice run. He pulled a hand out of his pocket and in it was a folded piece of paper. Here, he said.

Witi unfolded it and recognised his dad's writing and the drawing of a landscape. It was the first time anything had been taken out of that room and here it was in the middle of the city.

Look familiar? he asked. It should.

It's the same as Jordy's map, Witi said. Same spot.

This bay is sacred to me, and it's sacred to you. Your ancestors used to believe it held a special power. A doorway to a source of eternal energy. Enough to knock the balance of nature if given the chance.

Don't sound like surf talk anymore, Koro.

Your dad's destiny was to be there to protect us from it happening.

Witi looked at the map, at the x-marks scattered over it, and he suddenly wondered who was more insane – the guy who drew this or the one sitting next to him.

Your father went there, Koro said, last time the swell was big enough to expose the source.

Eight years ago? Witi asked.

Been there the whole time. He knew what he had to do. I reckon your dad got trapped on the other side somehow, on the spirit side. Koro poked Witi with a finger. And if I'm right, only one person can release him.

Witi smiled.

But it won't be easy, lad. There are others who know about it. And they've spent a lot of money and effort creating an imbalance in our climate to ensure the storms are so severe and the swells so large that the gateway stays open more often. Because now they have far better technology and machines and the bloody greed to… let's just say, *tap* into it. They don't understand the consequences. They're blindsided by their own egos. A race to be the next to sit on that power throne, huh? Yeah, the ongoing saga of humanity. The good news is, we're sitting here 'cos your old man did his job.

Witi folded the map back up, fingers pressed to the sharp edges. His …*job*?

There's an entrance here, like a door of sorts, that's entrusted to a very special person. It was your father's time. He was blessed with the gift to read and control sound vibrations. The ones water release.

Knew it the moment I saw him. Knew it when I saw you too. You need to go as well, lad, he said. Your wairua is telling you your time has come too. Heh, congratulations, lad, you're a key too. It's your destiny.

LAST CHANCE AND ALL THAT

Man, was Witi in a torn mood after that episode with Koro. He was feeling crap he didn't even know he had in his emotional repertoire. Dr Herbert may've been a douche but he *had* helped him learn to recognise certain thoughts. Weird thing was, Witi remembered telling him about the voices from the ocean. Witi *did* used to hear them as a kid. His dad made it seem as natural as breathing, like everyone could hear them. But Dr Herbert told his mum that was Witi's way of transferring grief. That it wasn't normal. That the ocean was not a substitute for human communication.

The thought of more sessions wore Witi down and he started to go along with the doctor's recommendations. The first time he came in from the surf and told his mum he didn't hear anything, she hugged him far longer than normal.

Ironically, Witi later learnt that the best way to self-medicate was to go surfing. Standing on the ocean's surface was way better than being under it. Riding waves was everything pro surfers said about it, stuff like:

My form of escapism, man.

Where I meditate, man.

Purifies the soul, man.

It's electrifying, man.

Yeah, nah. All of that, eh, but more like hangin' with the Big Guy at a table for two. Didn't matter what his problems were when he was that close. Each wave was a conversation. A dance. A game of chess. A surprise gift. The transfer of energy from one entity to another.

All of that, eh, but ...

Whatever, man.

Important thing, Witi believed, was that his footsteps back on the sand were always a little more spaced apart than those heading into the water.

Surfers were damn lucky to have a direct line to the Head Cheese like that.

But during one ice-cream, Koro had ripped the friggin' lid off that and what was once suppressed and self-managed now surged through Witi like a tsunami.

When Koro and Witi arrived back at the house, Jordy and Alana were there.

Jordy looked on edge – even more than usual – and Alana was sitting on the porch step with her knees tucked under her chin.

What you guys doin'? Witi asked.

Ol' man got home early, Jordy said. Had a bit of a barny with him. He pointed to Alana. She was here already.

Been thinking, Alana said. Last chance and all that.

They all stared at each other. Who was supposed to name what was on all their minds? So Koro made it easy and threw Jordy the keys to the Land Rover.

It's yours, take it. I keep some old sleeping bags in the back behind the seat too.

Cunning bugger, Koro.

Love to, but I didn't get time to grab my board, Jordy said. Just a wettie.

Koro motioned to the shed. Just happens to be a quiver in there, he said. Take ya pick.

But Koro ... Witi said.

They'll do the job, he replied.

Nah, wasn't meaning ...

These guys need you.

Witi looked at Jordy, already pulling the old man's surfboards down from the rafters and inspecting them. Alana was sticking her own in the back tray of the vehicle. She looked across at Witi.

What do we really have here, Witi? Another day at college? Even they don't want us. Let Jimmy and the rugby guys have the place. It'll all still be there when we get back. We belong at the beach – that's *our* turf.

She's right, Koro added. And your dad needs you.

Witi shook his head. Whole thing's nuts. Fuckin' crazy.

You're sounding like that doc of yours. And your mother.

She'll be home shortly. We'll talk to her then.

She won't allow it – you know that.

I have to try.

There's no time.

Koro.

Embrace it, lad – embrace your destiny. Your mates are already doing it for you.

Jordy had a board, the longest thruster he could find, and was placing it above Alana's. She was already sitting in the cab staring out the window at Witi. A fantail landed on the bonnet and flexed its wings.

You don't know for certain, Koro. How can you?

The bird knows, he said.

Witi looked back at him. His face tried to settle on an expression, but there wasn't one. Koro's was as steely as ever.

You know about that? But ...

He visits me too, lad. It's your father's mauri. Been watching you and me, eh.

Nah, Witi said. Pīwakawaka – it's a coincidence. They make ya think there's something special going on, but nah.

You sure lad? Certain?

Yeah. Found out in biology class they just want you to move so they can check out what dirt's been disturbed, what food your feet have unearthed.

Again with the experts, huh? That teacher doesn't know the half of it. The experts also said your father abandoned you both, but what if he's just waiting for you? What if he's trapped and you're the only one who can release him? What if you simply have to find him?

That's not possible. It's not normal.

Dr Herbert would be so proud of you at the moment.

Jordy honked the horn.

I can't leave Mum. She thinks this is all bullshit. It'll be too much.

I'll take care of it, Koro said, his tone now full of mana. She never wanted to listen — she hated the stories she heard as a child and refused to believe them as an adult. But this time she'll have to trust me for once. Trust you too. And give that bird more credit. It likes you.

PART III

INITIALS IN THE TREE

Piece of shit, said Jordy. Any time he tried to get the Land Rover into third gear it sounded like it had arthritis. Witi and Alana had to brace themselves against the dashboard as it stuttered and shrieked its way through the process.

Fark this, Jordy said and pulled over. You drive.

Witi found third sweet-as and Alana laughed.

He pulled into the first petrol station and while he filled the tank Alana and Jordy grabbed snacks.

Afterwards they sat alone in the left lane of the motorway and headed eastward towards the black fortress of cloud in the sky.

They followed the directions on Jordy's map. For a while Witi drove the vehicle along familiar roads, but when Jordy said to take the next right, Witi questioned him.

Unless you want to tramp down the coast for a day? Jordy responded.

Witi turned down the unnamed gravel road and they rattled along for well over an hour through valleys of farmland that transformed into dense scrub with not a fenceline in sight. An alertness filled the cab. The road itself degenerated into an overgrown track with rocks and potholes big enough to slow the journey another hour longer than expected. By now the needle on the temperature gauge was sitting in the red and Witi tapped the glass in hope it was only stuck there. But the steam leaking out one side of the bonnet was a give-away. Shortly after, the Land Rover lost its power and rolled to a stop.

Witi turned the key over a few times – C'mon, c'mon – but nothing happened. Out of frustration he punched the steering wheel and the truck tooted.

The other two stared at him like he was meant to come up with an alternative.

Looks like the walk's started then, Witi said.

And it looks like we're gonna be longer than we thought, Alana said. You guys gonna push this piece of shit back home afterwards?

While Witi was taking the green single-fin surfboard off the back tray he noticed a number. A small worn 800 etched in the blue paint. He didn't think much of it until he grabbed his bag and found it had been sitting on top of a 300. He spotted a faded 8 up by the back window too.

They walked in a line. Jordy had that bounce in his step again, like he wanted to be the first to see whatever was around the next corner. What was he expecting to find? According to the map they were yet to reach the block of bush. Witi's arms were aching already with the weight of a surfboard and a bag and he turned to see how Alana was feeling.

Tired already? she said as she strode past.

By now they could hear distant rumbling and Jordy said they must be getting close to hear thunder.

But all Witi was hearing was his name being faintly called in the deep tone.

The road was nothing more than a walking track now. It ran out at a wall of native bush. Heavy vegetation bore down all around them and Witi imagined the labyrinth within. Wondered how many circles they'd end up walking in, especially if ol' dingo was leading the way.

Map's gonna be useless in here, Jordy said.

First bit of sense Witi had heard from him, eh.

S'pose if we just head for the thunder, he continued.

Did Aussie's IQ rise when you left? Alana asked. Time for a new leader, she said pushing past him. My turn.

She stepped into the shadows and was consumed. Surfboard and all.

Jordy went to say something but nothing fell out. First time for everything, Witi guessed. Jordy had no choice but to follow her.

Witi took one last look at the fantail circling against the black canvas of sky and joined them.

The path was a faint noodle amongst the gnarly roots and foliage. And it was dark too; it took a while for their eyes to adjust. Was it even a proper track? Witi looked high above to where cracks of dull light entered through the nest of intertwined branches.

There seemed to be a different hiss and hum in here:

like they were under water – well, kinda.

Could breathe sweet, but

rata vines slowed them and snagged their surfboards like seaweed, and wildlife fled like fish.

Not like the ocean really, but

another world like that, eh?

Couldn't help feel the same affinity.

Witi's ancestral land.

They walked for ages, and when they slowed right up Jordy suggested they take a break to get their bearings. They chowed down a muesli bar each and for the first time thought about being lost.

Where's your mum? Alana blurted it out to Jordy.

Witi hadn't given her a heads-up so he braced himself for the look he was about to get.

She died a few years back.

Shit, I'm sorry. I shouldn't have ...

Nah, it's all good, he said. You weren't to know.

Filthy look right there.

She was a professor. An expert in mythology and cultures, links with modern science and stuff. Don't really know much about what she did specifically other than she died on a trip to Indonesia. A super bad strain of malaria. She loved surfing. Got me into it. We spread her ashes off Stradbroke Island, so that was pretty cool.

I'm sorry, Alana said again. She sounds like a wonderful woman.

Yeah, she was. Jordy looked away and his mouth tightened.

Alana gave him a hug and he embraced it—longer than appropriate. Alana was the first to break and Jordy made the shortest of eye contact with Witi. Alana walked over and scratched all their initials in a tree trunk with a sharp rock.

So anyone will know three waxheads were here, she said.

They checked their phones and each confirmed there was no service. Even Jordy's flash-as phone. Alana suggested they think about camping for the night. But Witi reckoned they couldn't be far from breaking through to the coast.

Could be better reception, he said.

Dunno 'bout that, Jordy said, his map out again. We're in this thick area of green. I reckon Alana's right.

Witi saw his wink. This time she showed Jordy her dimples and above them the sky flashed.

Nah, trust me, it's not far, Witi said. Should be just up this next ridge. He started walking away, desperately willing them to follow. When he turned they were trudging in his steps.

But he didn't know where he was going.

He was relying on guidance or a sign to get him through.

My ancestral land, eh?

He wasn't even sure why he pushed it to be honest.

Just, he couldn't let Jordy call all the shots. Or wink whenever he wanted.

Nah, never been the jealous type.

Yet he couldn't stop walkin'.

And after a further hour of it, now in the aged light and heavy rain, Witi wished he hadn't opened his big mouth. Wished he'd never seen that wink.

Especially when Jordy stopped and made sure every living thing in the forest was aware that they were passing, their initials carved in the tree trunk.

Yeah, Jordy and Alana were pretty pissed with Witi, eh.

He was pissed with himself.

And he felt a fresh swell of emotion inside him.

Full of grazed white caps scalped by internal wind.

And he went real quiet-like, yeah.

Alana would normally have seen this. Heck, her presence would normally still the waters by default. But she had that look going on, it seemed she was over this adventure. They faced reality and started to prepare for a night out, just like how those hiking deaths start out. Another statistic in the dumb ways to die list. At least they had matches. Jordy had found them in the glovebox of the Land Rover and figured they could be handy.

Witi couldn't meet his eyes.

Sitting back against a tree, legs tucked under his surfboard acting as a roof, he looked across at Jordy and Alana sharing Jordy's opened sleeping bag under their two boards fixed tightly between rata vines. Her head perilously close to resting on his shoulder.

After a few half-hearted minutes of life the fire faded and darkness drowned them. The hiss and hum changed to a violent howl and the rain sounded like sprays of gunfire as it rode in on the surges of wind.

But it was nothing on what had built inside Witi.

He couldn't sleep, and when he did he dreamt of his mum in tears on the kitchen floor and Koro standing over her laughing, both oblivious to the soldiers marching towards them and his own screams from the murky blackness of the ocean floor.

Worst night of his life, eh.

FELT LIKE A GOOFY

Witi gasped for breath.

His eyes struggled to focus on the movement around him. When they did he saw Alana and Jordy looking at him like he was just another problem.

You okay? Alana shouted over the noise of the wind screaming above them. All around, tree limbs groaned and strained under the force.

Are you okay? she shouted again.

He raised a thumb and pushed the green surfboard off his lap. He braced himself upright against the tree. He was saturated and hotter than a Land Rover engine.

Watch it! Jordy yelled.

Witi ducked as a branch big enough to smash his skull swung in the air and exploded against the tree behind him. He crawled the short distance to the other two sheltering behind a large trunk.

There was fear in Alana's eyes, or uncertainty at least. He couldn't tell – she'd never shown it before so this look was new to him. She flinched with each crack, crash or boom that seemed to rattle every blood cell in their bodies. But Jordy had a grin not even this wind could blow away.

What's funny? Witi asked.

It's a farkin' cyclone, man. We're in a cyclone!

You're insane, Witi said.

We're insane, he said pointing a finger three ways.

We need to get back, Alana said. I want to get back—this is stupid.

What for? Jordy said. We're this far.

We're gonna die out here.

She's right, Witi said.

Nah, we'll be sweet.

Nearby a tree broke in a series of snaps, then cracks from the domino effect on other trees in its fall. The earth shook as it struck the ground.

Alana jumped to her feet. I'm out of here, she said.

Alana and Witi packed, scrambling their gear together. Jordy did the same, but Witi knew he was looking for any excuse to head on towards the ocean.

Alana's bag was tightly tied to her back and she held her board in both hands like she was ready to use it as a shield at any second. Witi didn't know if she knew where she was going. But they all just started running that way.

The forest floor struggled to hold the amount of rain falling and a massive network of small rivers ran like veins towards the bottom of the valley. Problem was, Witi had feet perfect for the top of a surfboard,

paddles destined for surfing, the old man used to tell him, but ...

Sure, he could walk on water, make a surfboard do whatever whenever.

But on land he felt like he was stuck in goofy shoes at the best of times.

Felt like a goofy.

So he stayed off playing fields and courts and avoided team sports.

And in this muddy confusion

he slipped,

got to his feet, carried on,

and slipped again, while Alana built on the distance between them.

She couldn't hear his yelling, eh.

She was too light-footed, and the last Witi saw was her hair trailing like a flag until that too was digested by all the brown and green.

And he slipped yet again.

This time he and his board slid metres down the hill until he wrapped himself around a tree. He tried to stand and looked like he was caught in an oil slick. Jordy came sliding down the same mud surge. He was bigger than Witi and carried more momentum. He missed the tree, slammed into Witi's shins and the two of them continued downhill to the sound of Witi's grunts and Jordy's cheering. The veins of water turned into full arteries of sodden soil that sped them on. Sometimes they bounced from tree to tree like a gauntlet run. Other times they bounced off each other or were threatened with the sharp fins and pointed noses of their surfboards which they were no way going to let go. They were a couple of bits of debris being flushed away.

The soaked dirt gave way to a waterfall and they fell through open air ... and landed side by side. Witi sank into a mass of dirt-brown bubbles. He gained enough perspective to kick to the surface and swim to the shallows. Jordy was sitting on the riverbank already. Even through his mask of mud Witi saw his front teeth shining at him.

They argued for a long time after that.

Mainly over the uncertainty of the situation. At least they agreed on one thing: to find Alana as quick as they could. But they had no patience for each other's suggestions. Jordy's idea was to scale the waterfall and try and retrace their steps. That grin of his didn't last long. Witi watched him scratch and slip his way up and down the embankment, never once getting further than halfway while Witi hurled abuse at him. The last time Jordy tried he came crashing down again into the swollen river amongst pieces of roots and branches, and Witi reckoned his tantrum afterwards almost calmed the wind.

He walked past Witi still puffing.

C'mon, man, you gave it a good crack, Witi said. He didn't mean it to sound that patronising.

Get farked.

Witi figured they should head upriver in that hope that Alana had ended up down here as well. But after a short walk Jordy took satisfaction in pointing out that the river actually veered away in a direction nowhere near where they'd been. So they headed back to where they'd started.

Lucky, huh? Jordy said. Didn't feel much like walking in circles again anyway.

Get fucked.

So they sat on the bank with their sodden bags and surfboards, throwing stones into the river and watching it grow wider, faster and browner. Waiting for a better solution.

Did Witi have any muesli bars left?

Nope.

Did Jordy still have his map?

He pointed to a soaked mess of paper on a rock.

You love her? Jordy asked.

The words were the quietest spoken in the last couple of hours yet they pierced through the noise of their world ending louder than anything said previously. Witi looked across at Jordy.

Do you love her? Jordy repeated, ignoring eye contact by throwing another stone in the water.

Yeah, sure.

You say it like a gay guy talking about his best girlfriend.

Fuck off.

Just didn't sound convincing, that's all.

What happened last night? Witi asked.

Nothin'.

Nothin'?

Nothin', he said. Well, you're not admitting you're stuck in the friend-zone so I'm just telling you before I make my next move.

Eh?

You know, best to be straight-up about these things. No hard feelings.

Witi's next stone hit Jordy's head.

So Jordy threw one back.

They met halfway and wrestled to the ground. Witi doubted either of them would throw a punch, not in the situation they were in, but there had to be a victor. For a moment Jordy had the best of him, and Witi's noodles were no match for Jordy's thick arms. But Witi was quick, and when he broke free he tripped Jordy and wrapped his arms around his neck. He pressed Jordy's face into the stony ground until he stopped squirming and tapped out with his hand.

She's my girlfriend, Witi said. And, yeah, you're cutting my grass.

She know that? Jordy said, his voice wheezy and muffled. 'Cos I think she's a little confused.

Hey! they heard. Hey!

He released Jordy and together they stared at the river, watching the vision appear. Alana in her wetsuit was floating down on her surfboard; the fantail darting ahead of her swooped vertical and caught the next wind gust away. She paddled frantically to the side before she was swept around the next corner.

Man, am I stoked to see you guys!

CEASE ITS RAGE

When Alana reached Witi she clung to him.

I was freakin' out, she said. Didn't think I'd see you guys again.

Witi stroked her back and didn't try to move her wet hair out of his face. He whispered they were worried too and that he'd protect her, promise.

We'll protect you, Jordy said as he rummaged in her bag. He pulled out two muesli bars and held them up as if they were a couple of winning Lotto tickets. And just like that his grin was back.

Alana had a theory the only way to guarantee an exit out of the forest was to follow the river to the sea. From there, she had no idea what to expect, but surely a rescue from an aerial search would be far more likely on the coast than out of sight. Jordy and Witi shared a look and resisted being the first to acknowledge the logic.

Jordy and Witi stripped off to get into their wetsuits. Alana didn't try and turn or anything; she busied herself putting everything she could into one bag. Witi didn't muck around. He'd had enough of this spot and was keen to move on before the earth opened up and swallowed them. But Jordy's wetsuit was inside out and when Witi looked up, Jordy was milking his moment of nakedness in front of Alana for all it was worth.

Posing like he was the friggin' statue of David.

Flexing what he could while he slowly moved fingers in and out of the limbs of his wettie.

Hands like a wrestler, eh.

Alana finished what she was doing and looked up in time for an eyeful.

While trees crashed and the river rose and the wind and rain raged hell around them.

He could pick his moments for good effect, Witi'd give him that.

Witi zipped up, lifted his surfboard, and waded into the current.

When you guys have finished playing ladies' night, he called back.

The river moved them quickly. There were plenty of obstacles to navigate, mostly logs and giant branches lurching up beside and under their boards. At one point a fallen tree straddled the full width of the river, a massive elder of the forest. They approached it fast as they bobbed along with the pulse of the water. They manoeuvred to the only obvious gap that was channelling water between the mass of broken branch fingers. Everywhere else the river hit the tree and formed heaves of angry brown chaos.

Jordy got through first, but Alana didn't quite make the opening. Her board was instantly sucked under the tree. She scragged at branches as the water lashed her face. Witi was right behind her but his hand couldn't reach her in time. The branch suddenly broke and she disappeared. Through the gap he could see the shock on Jordy's face as he tried vainly to paddle back up the river.

In the panic, Witi's board went horizontal to the opening, closing off the gap. And he was thrown into the surge too.

He sucked in what air he could as he went under.

And the solid feel of thick branches caged him in somewhere under the tree.

As the water pinned him like a stick in a giant filter.

Couldn't see past the black and brown,

past the stupidity of it all.

He was gonna die here.

And he thought about who of his ancestors had done the same and how.

Was he the dumbest of them all?

Weird shit like that in the space of a mere second.

Fuckin' stupidity of it.

He felt around in the brown and black for an opening

And felt Alana's limp hand outstretched like she'd been waiting and got bored.

He clasped it and pulled but there was no yielding.

He thrashed and strained at the barriers between them but

it was an elder of the forest – it'd survived his ancestors.

So with the last of his breath Witi yelled at the water instead.

He told it to stop, told it to cease its raging.

Just for a moment.

One small moment.

And with his hands he pushed the water back upstream.

And the water backed up.

Enough for him to pluck Alana's tangled, lifeless body from the branches.

Yeah, the tree's fingers had her pinned real good.

But in one merciful moment he pulled her out

and carried her to the safety of land.

He didn't even notice the water return to its frenzy.

Witi checked her breathing. Her pulse. Neither were there. His training kicked in. Her lips were soft and still warm and if this was any other time Witi would've been the happiest guy around.

He pumped her chest with his palm and counted the repetitions in his head. He stared at her face for the slightest flicker from her curled eyelashes. But all he got was the sickening nod of her head each time his hands pressed down.

C'mon, babe, c'mon.

He opened her mouth and pushed his breath as far down her throat he could, feeling her stomach rise each time. He locked his fingers and resumed pumping her chest. Her ribs and sternum felt like they were cracking under the pressure but if it meant her eyelashes moved then he didn't care.

Babe, c'mon.

Babe.

Jesus, babe, wake up!

Jordy was here. Witi couldn't see him but he could feel his silent presence as he sat and watched.

Alana started coughing out water. She opened her eyes but they stared right through Witi as he yelled in her face and rolled her on her side. Witi never knew the human body could hold that much liquid. Doubted Jordy did either. They watched it snaking its way back to the river as her breathing returned, faint but steady.

You okay? Witi pulled her hair away from her face.

Her head moved but only just.

Jordy passed him a bag—something soft to put under her head—and when Witi looked at him, instead of his grin, he was staring like Witi was the one with the problem.

They didn't leave her side and made her as comfortable as they could. They spoke to her—softly and reassuringly—and while she never answered, her eyes seemed to gain a little more focus as the moments went on. Jordy tried to light a fire but nothing was dry. He snapped glances at Witi as he paced back and forth. He went through the box of matches and when the last one puffed out with the latest gust of wind he swore and threw sticks at the sky. When he saw the fantail sitting in a tree next to them he wanted to know what the fuck it was looking at. Witi figured he was in shock, like he was; guessed it was his way of dealing with it. Just a boisterous Aussie.

He and Witi made another roof and sourced branches for shelter and afterwards, with Alana between them, they huddled close until darkness found them again.

Witi, she said, the words barely audible over the weather.

Yeah, he said. Yeah?

Told you ... don't call me babe.

He held her hand and she held it back.

TELL 'ER WHAT YOU DID

In the haze of the early morning, Alana ate the last muesli bar. Jordy and Witi stared at the wrapper collecting raindrops. When Alana told them her chest was sore Witi was so happy she was eating and talking that he told her it was just a bit of bruising, nothing more.

What happened to me? she asked. I don't remember much more than a tree blocking the river.

Witi looked across at Jordy and saw that the night hadn't taken that cynical look from him.

He answered her before Witi had a chance.

You got swept underneath it. Dead-set goner.

How'd I get out?

Yeah, Witi, how'd she get out? Cos I'm a little vague on that and I saw the whole thing.

Witi shrugged. I swam under and got you, I guess. No biggie.

Yeah ... dunno about that, Jordy said. Seemed like the river stopped.

Dunno what you're ...

Something made that angry bastard of water chill the hell out. That's how he got you.

Stopped? she said, showing a hint of dimple. Whaddya mean?

You know, like a duck pond. A swimming pool. Once he got you outta there the place went apeshit again.

Witi didn't know what to say. He'd already spent the night trying to rationalise the way his hallucinations had jumped from annoying mind-games to reality.

Alana was looking out of the shelter and shaking her head at the tree now almost completely submerged with the night's extra rain. Probably imagining herself stuck underneath it.

You did that? she said.

I don't really know what I did.

Witi, your dad, she said. Your dad said he could talk —

The old man was crazy, and so was I for thinking he could be out here. We should never've come.

But doesn't this explain it?

Explain what? asked Jordy. He looked from one to the other. When they didn't answer, he asked again: You guys, explain what?

Alana started to tell him about the diary and Witi's dad and his special gift with the ocean. When she stopped to rest her throat, Witi filled in the gaps, mindful that each word would only make him and his dad sound like classic loony bin candidates. It was unlikely Jordy could even start to comprehend the scale of it all. Witi's dad's life seemed to have been one part movie script, one part rock opera, and while Aussie may be a big place it'd probably never produced anyone with a life quite like his old man's. By the time Witi finished, Jordy's face was dead set in denial.

Came from the ocean? he said.

An international superstar?

Could talk to water?

On some sorta spiritual mission?

Your dad?

Nah, I'm callin' bullshit. But, Jordy chuckled, but, yeah. Funny thing is, here I am desperate enough to run from my old man that I'd head straight into the middle of the biggest cyclone in history. And here you are, so desperate to find yours, you'd do the same. Mate, had me fooled. Shoulda known you weren't in it for braggin' rights.

Koro reckons it's my destiny.

Riding giant waves? Don't think so.

Nah, doing what Dad's doing.

Which is?

Witi shrugged. He wished he had an answer for everything. He wished he could say to Jordy and Alana, *This is why I'm here. This is what I have to do.* But he could only look at them both like he was getting yelled at by the old man for leaving the door open while his maps blew from one end of the room to the other.

Hmph, thought so, Jordy said. Might wanna tell your pop to lay off the ganga next time, huh?

They were lost.

This was the conclusion they all came to. None of them had the motivation or the energy to confidently say they could lead the other two to safety. And safety was now at the top of their priority list. Some food at least. But they were so lost they went nowhere. They wanted the wind to stop, the rain to chill the hell out. It felt like being stuck in a detuned radio. Jordy went on about the whole river episode again and, try as he might, the only answer he could come up with was that Witi was a freak.

Witi got up and walked off.

Ya don't even need an umbrella, Jordy yelled.

Let it go, Witi heard Alana say.

He walked until there were enough trees separating them and peeled his wetsuit off so he could take a leak. Afterwards, he began retracing his steps. He stopped at a large puddle and saw his face amongst the pin drops of water with their tiny rings of energy like mini-lows on a weatherman's map. He checked to confirm the others weren't in sight. Then he rubbed his hands together while he focused on the water.

So deep and hard, his eyes felt like they'd pop out of their sockets and splash at his feet.

He aimed his hands at the surface as if he was some sort of wizard about to ...

He was gonna ...

Like he wanted to ...

The water was about to ...

Yeah, nah, he didn't know what was gonna happen, eh. Didn't

know what he was capable of. Apparently he'd stopped a raging river. And here he was failing to tame a puddle. Move it, flatten it, something, anything.

And still the rain fell. He felt stupid for even believing it himself.

Just a dude with goofy feet, and hands on the ends of noodles.

Pal.

He ignored it the first time. There were a lot of noises out here, could've been anything. But then:

Pal.

Pal.

He turned in circles, trying to catch where it came from. It came from everywhere, carried on the swirling wind, like every drop of rain had his name reverberating inside it. Ripples of sound like drips in a puddle.

Pal.

A silhouetted figure stood perfectly framed between two giant tree trunks.

Dad?

Yeah, pal. Yeah.

Witi walked towards him, his chest struggling to process the excited breaths, but the figure kept at the same distance. So Witi ran. He leapt over fallen trees and crouched under branches. At times he lost sight of his dad, only for the dark outline to appear again, but every time in a slightly different direction.

Dad! Wait!

But he never did.

Can't have heard him or something. Witi was yelling into a cyclone.

Eventually Witi's body refused to keep up with no fuel in it, and he was forced to stop and lean against a stump to catch his breath. His dad was nowhere to be seen. Witi stood up on the stump but all he could see were brown stripes and fine green ferns being thrown around in the wind. Any emotions still under his control broke free and he yelled:

You leave us wondering for eight fuckin' years and now you want to play games?! Screw you! Screw you! You fuckin' deserter! He punched two middle fingers into the air and yelled bastard until his throat felt raw and his eyes swelled with tears.

Fuck you, he sobbed. His voice now quiet. We don't need you anyway.

Witi couldn't say how long he stayed there. He'd lost touch with time and hope. He sat and stared at the sludge on the ground and the water channelling off his fringe and cheeks. Felt numb. Like he didn't give a damn about anything. Nothing was worth it. For a while even the sound of the machine-gun rain and the chill gusts of wind couldn't penetrate him. He closed his eyes and prepared to accept whatever his so-called destiny had for him.

His name was the first thing that broke through.

Witi.

Like the bass in a rock ballad. It shook the forest floor with every call.

And he felt a tingle right in his bones.

Yeah, he'd heard that voice before, but never so deep, so full of power.

It brought him back to the present. He opened his eyes.

He stood and stepped towards the calling voice. This time there was no rush, no scratches from low-hanging branches or close calls. He waded through a thick wall of fern and suddenly the forest ended. He had to grab handfuls of vegetation to brace himself against the full force of the wind.

Witi was at the edge of a cliff, overlooking a large beach cove below. And he instantly knew from its shape that this was where they were meant to be all along.

THE EYE OF IT

Witi was still puffing from running all the way back, but he was smiling with the best news they'd had all day.

Jordy saw him first: Where the hell you been?

Alana groaned and rolled her eyes and shook her head all at the same time. She must've been worried.

I've seen the bay. We've been close the whole time.

Good one, Jordy said. Come to you in a dream, did it?

Nah, honest.

You found it, Alana said, and made it back here without getting lost?

He nodded, wanting the right words to shake out, but he couldn't dress it up. So he told them the truth.

The old man showed me the way. My own footsteps in the mud got me back.

Jordy sniggered and looked away.

Alana sat back against the tree.

Jesus, Witi. C'mon, she said.

Witi stared up at the ragged patches of sky. He stayed there catching raindrops in his mouth and watching the tips of trees move like the front row of a heavy rock concert. Man, he wanted the wind to stop, the rain to hold up. Just enough so he could think clearly for a moment. Instead, he figured what the hell. Apparently he was only a pair of sandals away from what Moses did with water. As far as Alana and Jordy were concerned, Witi couldn't get any weirder.

And I s'pose you got into the river by yourself when you were lost? he blurted to Alana.

She shrugged lightly. Pretty much. It seemed logical at the time.

So that fantail had nothing to do with it?

You saw that bird? I was just looking for any sign. Had nothing to lose, it was the only other living thing around.

It's been with us since we left the city, he said. Don't you remember seeing it? I thought I was going crazy but it's been with me since Dad left.

Oh, man – c'mon, guys, give me break! Jordy interrupted.

Eight years it's been like a guardian to me. Koro's seen one too.

It's just a farkin' bird, mate.

Nah, Jordy, it's the old man's mauri. His energy, guiding me. Witi pointed at Alana. Guided you too.

I did end up finding you guys,

but …

Yeah. Yeah, you did.

And Jordy, remember that moment in the hallway? Back at my house? You freaked out 'cos I lost it?

Yeah.

You were my old man. He was reaching to me and I was reaching back.

Oh, right. Maaate, shoulda said so at the time.

Yeah, Witi said. Yeah, probably should've. But I thought you'd... well, you know. I thought it was just another hallucination.

Jordy turned to Alana. He always like this when he doesn't take his medication?

Bro, only thing I'm taking is this. Witi ripped his board from the shelter and stuck it under his arm. Good luck, Jordy. C'mon, Alana, at least I'm doin' something.

But they both followed him, surfboards and all.

Witi felt a bit of vindication return. They hadn't trusted him to come back for them, eh. They were paying more attention to their surroundings, though. Looking for ghosts, he guessed.

But even he didn't see his dad again, just his own footprints from the previous trek still visible for the others. When he stood back and waved them through the last mass of fern, he took great pleasure in the cries of joy blasted back to him on the wind.

As he felt the earth move with every call of his name.

They slid down the steep hill under thick, sheltering, wind-strong tussock. It spat them onto the beach where instead of feeling soft sand under their feet, their neoprene skins were blasted. Sand found its way into every opening and they were forced back to the vegetation. They shielded behind their surfboards, which one by one were blown out of their hands and would've been lost in the clouds without the legropes around their wrists. Alana tried to tame hers as it spun in the air like a fish lure.

There! Witi yelled, pointing. Behind those rocks!

And they began crawling towards them.

They sat with their backs pressed to a boulder face, spitting out what sand they could. Behind the cluster of giant stones was more solid and dry than they'd felt for a while. Even a cyclone couldn't move this formation. For a moment Witi let his eyes close and he imagined he was back in his house listening to a train rattling past his bedroom window.

And he wished that train would stop and take them far from here.

Then it did stop. Witi didn't know how long they'd waited.

But it did.

The wind.

The rain.

The noise.

They looked up from deep within their stony burrow and suddenly they had a growing blue ceiling.

What the fark?

And Jordy was right.

But the silence wasn't complete; still the ground shook with every syllable of Witi's name.

They walked outside. There was no sand in the air. They could hear their own breathing. They squinted against the bright sunshine and tried to make sense of it. A small herd of seals was appearing from between reef boulders. They yelped like excited kids as a couple of larger seals made their way to the water's edge. Encircling them, in the distance, the cyclone was still raging in a smoky black cloud. It was like being inside a giant stadium kilometres wide.

Must be the eye of it, Alana said quietly.

They no longer had to yell, but neither Jordy nor Witi was registering. If a fire alarm had blared behind them Witi doubted they would've answered. They stood shoulder to shoulder watching the ocean, a solid paddle away – but doable – rising into a giant rolling slab that captured every piece of sunlight in its pale-green skin, before the whole face darkened as it folded upon itself. It was hard to comprehend how thick that mass of falling water must be, but the trembling of the beach beneath their feet as the wave ignited in white-water told them something.

Wi-ti

Wi-ti

The wave in perfect formation.

No sooner did it rise and appear, than it was killing itself with its own energy.

Sparkled green,

Shadowed,

White.

Witi sensed Jordy's arms flex then drop; he was already going through the motions of surfing it.

And suddenly the last day's drama, their hunger and despair and fear of the unknown, all lost significance.

You call it, Jordy said.

Ten. Maybe twelve feet, Witi said.

They watched another one, coulda been its identical twin.

Wi-ti

That's gotta be a solid twelve, he said.

Alana stood beside Witi.

Yeah, they're nice waves, she said, but, guys, c'mon.

Your pop was right, Jordy said, and his voice didn't have any of the rasp Witi'd got used to. This is perfection, he said.

Alana looked at them both before settling on Witi.

Witi?

Wi-ti

How long you think we got? Jordy asked.

Dunno, Witi said, but he was already thinking it. Couldn't help himself. Only a surfer knows the feeling, eh. Could be half an hour, maybe more? he said. What the hell.

Then I'm out there. Jordy started running back to the boulders for his board.

Alana was hanging back, but Witi knew by the look on her face what she wanted to say.

Sorry, just one wave, eh? he smiled. We're here.

She shook her head and pursed her lips in an exhale. She rubbed her sternum and Witi knew that whatever pain she felt was already being eclipsed as she watched the next wave.

Honestly, just a taste.

Don't think I'm stayin' on the beach while you boys kiss and make up out there.

Yeah, course. Whatever, babe.

WHADDYA WAITIN' FOR?

They waded out to knee deep and felt the shove and tug and suck of confused water. There was so much energy being trapped in this cove: after the water hit the foreshore it was forced to the perimeters of the reef where it regrouped and was channelled back out to sea in a series of rapids. It was this rip that carried them out faster than they'd ever be able to paddle and let them arrive at the impact zone of the reef with barely a drop of water in their hair. Once there, with the dark three-storey walls of water rolling towards them, they had to rely on their own power to escape the impact zone. Their hands crabbed through the water as they paddled for the channel of calmer water beside the reef. One by one they moved skyward as the wave's tail caught and heaved beneath them. Witi looked over his shoulder at the eye of the thundering barrel staring back at him.

Yeah, nah, fifteen feet was an understatement.

Easy twenty, eh.

Then throw in that power they'd all just experienced.

He'd surfed all types, but ...

This thing was like, *whoa*, eh.

It was concentrated energy.

It had its own soul. He felt it.

Felt somethin', anyway.

A kinda pull towards it. A definite push away.

Kept paddling.

He heard a hundred whispered conversations come to a sudden stop.

The same voices as the other day. No way it was a coincidence.

Still paddling, all three of them, shoulders burning.

After the last couple of days all sorts of crazy was becoming the norm.

He couldn't wait to get over the top of this lot, to some sense of safety.

But Jordy was hollering, like a mad outback redneck teasing the biggest bull ever.

The three of them sat in the channel and watched the next few waves come in and fall in the same spot, all with the same theatrical grace.

Devastation still raging around them, 'cept here, right now.

They were sitting, semi-submerged on their boards in the middle of the stadium.

In the eye of the storm.

And the waves were putting on a performance with ...

yeah, the theatrical grace of someone centre-stage.

Calling them out from the wings ... where Witi was tossing up whether to hit it or watch a couple more.

For now, anyway.

But Jordy ...

Man, Jordy.

He'd seen enough and was paddling away towards the take-off zone.

You guys comin'? he asked over his shoulder.

Witi looked at Alana.

Might just watch a few, eh? she said.

Then I'll hang back to keep you company, Witi lied, and stroked his hands through the ocean to get closer to her.

Pussy! Jordy shouted back when he didn't get an answer.

They watched another set of waves come in and break.

The whispers. His name. That weird feeling. Every time.

You hear that? he asked Alana.

Hear what?

Nah, nothin'.

Four waves went by while Jordy paddled up and around the zone, to the left, and frantically to the right, trying to find the best spot to latch into one. He was lifted and dragged, and somehow each time cheated his way out of being thrown backwards with the falling lip of the wave. When he crawled over the top of the next one they lost sight of him for ages. Then, he appeared, his board pointing towards land, Jordy scrambling and kicking his way into the final largest wave of the set. In its last moments it grew another third its size and as Jordy committed to his feet, he shrank in comparison. Especially when it swallowed him like he was a piece of plankton.

Alana gasped.

Witi let out a groan.

They waited for him to reappear, waiting for it to go either way.

The wave spat white vapour from its barrel and Jordy shot out with it, body taut in classic surfer pose, like he was glued there. The reef guided the wave towards, then past them, and Jordy let out a war cry that lasted as long as the wave, then in various forms as he paddled back to them.

Fark, mate, whaddya waitin' for? he said without stopping. It's ya destiny, ain't it?

And just like that, dingo had gained a whole new level of attitude.

Alana followed Witi. He never asked if she was okay with it, but one look at her told him he didn't have to. He'd surfed with her enough to know that the arched back and wild, staring eyes were signs that she wouldn't answer anyway. But these waves were out of even her league. Western Aussie might've prepared Jordy for this, but to Kiwis these were like marauding Vikings on a foreign shore.

Next one's yours, Aquaman. Jordy moved out of the way to give Witi priority

as the horizon gave birth to another collection of thin black lines.

Marching towards land

capturing the sunlight as the first wave inhaled, and grew and grew in height.

Marching towards them.

How could something with that much mass be so quiet?

Go! he heard from somewhere.

Coulda been Jordy or Alana, or his dad standing barefoot on the water behind them watching the wave,

waves all marching towards him and starting to turn to shadow.

And he turned, man.

He turned and paddled into that massive beast like it *was* his damn destiny.

A MOVING CAR IN THE NIGHT

The first sound he heard from the wave was the chatter of the surf-board slapping the water under him as it struggled to catch a rail. His hands shot up with the vertical rush, as if he was in an armed hold-up. Felt like his toes were the only thing holding him to the fibreglass; the stale wax on it was about as sticky as wet plastic. The bottom of the wave never seemed to get any closer until it suddenly did and he was almost knocked off balance by the thunderous crashing behind him when the wave began to implode. He reached the smooth flat water only to follow it in a long bottom-turn back up into the rolling wall as his board was sucked up the face. He set a line with the surfboard, the top of the wave curled and threw up all over him and he was transported into a roaring, swirling, beautiful open chasm.

By far the biggest barrel of his life, but ...

Yeah, coulda been just like the tube rides the pros got. Shoulda been a classic moment, but ...

inside the wave were the voices, and this time they weren't whispering. They were all trying to talk to him at once.

Nah, couldn't make out a single word, eh.

And his body started tingling like pins and needles and when his inside hand brushed the wall of the wave he swore he saw sparks trail behind and get recycled into the violent white wash. As his hand moved from side to side to keep him standing, particles of water sprang from the wave and followed its motions.

The voices chanted:

Wi-ti

Wi-ti

There was the oval eye of the opening as it circled.

Musta been.

Had to be the same, eh. What Father O had seen all those years ago.

He reached out to it, couldn't help himself.

The eye, eh.

But the wave pushed him straight through it in a rush of fine spray and he was in the warm light of the sun again. Only for the wave to run out of tide and decide to close out right down the line. He had nowhere to go but straight for the shore and hope that whatever terror of water was behind couldn't chase him down.

Didn't need to worry 'bout that, though.

The great wedge of water hit him straight in the head.

Felt like a block building falling on him.

Thought he'd been decapitated.

But when he felt himself smack the surface and bounce against the reef, and when there was a bright flash in his vision as his head thumped against the jagged rock, and the wave rag-dolled him, then, yeah nah, didn't make it any better.

He didn't know which way was up, and up was where he needed to be. His last breath had been blown out with the impact. He reached to his ankle for the legrope so he could start climbing up to his board which – due to its buoyant nature and him as its anchor – would be doing its best impression of a tombstone on the surface about now.

But all he felt in the tumbling darkness was a limp piece of plastic cord attached to his ankle. Nothing to link him back to the top. His ears started stinging the deeper he went. What whiteness he did see was fading like the taillights of a moving car in the night.

And he saw pictures of his life:

Holding Dad's neck in the surf.

Stepping off that first wave and giving him the biggest smile ever.

Mum in the garden, stopping to look across at Dad under the tree, and Witi on the branch above struggling to read what his dad was writing.

Mum crying on the kitchen floor.

Weeds choking flowers,

suffocating them.

Sunlight going.

Dying under all the darkness.

Blackest black he'd ever seen.

Black scribbles,

nothing but thick black energy …

Nah, neither of them was gonna get back to the surface again.

Witi heard the voices before he felt the hands. They told him he was gonna survive because, yeah.

He was being lifted, and with that the blackness transformed to grey, then silver as light mingled with the froth of broken white-water. That first inhale was like being born again, except for the vomiting and gagging and gulping as he treaded water, now out in the channel and still hundreds of metres away from the shore. Through tears forced from his eyes by the pressure he could just make out Alana drawing long, safe arches across her wave with the beauty of a gold-medal skater on an ice rink.

A hard object bumped the back of his head. He scragged onto his surfboard, trying not to wonder how it was even possible that he'd surfaced right next to it. He lay on his stomach, hands dangling in the water, face to one side, and repeated the words he'd been told somewhere in the depths far below:

The son of him.

He recognised the sound of the repetitive splashes approaching him.

You all right? Alana placed a hand on his back.

Just a bad close-out.

We didn't think you were gonna surface.

Got stuck in the spin cycle, eh. He sat up on his board and their eyes were level. He felt warm liquid flowing down his neck.

Geez, Witi, you're bleeding bad.

He touched his temple and looked at his hand. Red in his palm.

A hit of reality. A sudden reminder of where they were. Feeling the rise and fall of the swell beneath them. Alana was still staring at the wound and he guessed she was in that same space.

It's nuthin', he said, spinning his board towards shore. But you should stay here. Catch another one like your last.

It was beautiful, huh?

Best ever.

Then why ruin it? Looking back out at the horizon to Jordy, she stuck two fingers in her mouth, let out a shrill whistle to get his attention, and pointed energetically to the beach. Then Witi and Alana began the long paddle back in.

RUNNIN' AGAINST THE WIND

Jordy walked up the beach shortly after them, bringing the first gust of onshore wind with him, and dug the tip of his surfboard into the sand.

He high-fived them. Worth it, huh?

But his voice was now back to that throaty level they'd used in competing with the noise of the gusts. Behind him the ocean was turning back into a mess of crumbling swell and white water. Jordy's surfboard was blown over. The sun disappeared, leaving Jordy's white-toothed smile the brightest thing on the beach. They scrambled for their boards when the next gust of wind sent them airborne and cartwheeling.

They moved back into the rocky room. Outside the wind began to scream all around them, like they were stuck in the middle of a banshee convention. Cyclone Trudy was probably pissed at their lack of respect. Three teenagers out frolicking in the ocean while she turned her back to catch her breath. Couldn't help thinking they'd stirred her up. Guessed she was out for revenge.

They had to get out of here.

Yeah, the others agreed with that.

They agreed that Jordy would lead the way and on the count of three they made a run for it.

Witi was last to leave. Alana took two steps outside and her surfboard flew from her hands. It spiralled away with the wind like it was an autumn-dry leaf.

Trudy tried to take his too, at the same spot, but Witi gripped it so hard his fingers burned.

The old man made this board dance once, he thought.

And he was thrown about like a ship with its sail up at the wrong time.

He was too skinny with not enough meat on his bones.

Not like dingo and his statue of David bulk.

Witi saw Jordy's thick arm still around his board and Alana's hand clutching his other wrist, as he led her away into a cloud of sand and sea spray. That was the last thing he saw. Couldn't see shit after that.

Definitely couldn't see where he was going.

Goofy feet kept him upright, but that was about it.

He tried to follow their footsteps, but ...

Yeah, Trudy blew sand to cover their tracks. To mess with him.

'Cos she was pissed and all that.

So he ran straight even though he was blind and for all he knew going no straighter than a dog chasing its tail.

And he became disorientated.

In the terror, howls and pain of a million sand particles blasting his skin, he heard,

Pal

Hey, Pal.

This way.

Yeah, Pal, that's it.

He stumbled. He tripped over. He got back on one knee, then both feet.

He'd never felt all that stable on land at the best of times, yet here he was. Face pressed to the board and too afraid to stop moving his feet. Runnin' against the wind.

Something grabbed his arm and was pulling him on. In his blindness he just kept moving until at last there was vegetation under his feet.

He was back in the sanctuary of thick scrub and bracken. Jordy and Alana were staring at him, Jordy's hand still grasping Witi's bicep.

Stick with us next time, he yelled over the wind.

Witi looked down. The tips of his fingers were bleeding where they'd broken through the thick layer of green fibreglass.

EYES LIKE OCEAN CURRENTS

They squeezed past trees and stumbled over exposed roots. Witi led, but he didn't tell the other two he was following his old man.

Well, his voice anyway.

Not after what had happened.

Nah, wasn't worth it.

Funny thing was, Witi didn't hear them ask either, where they were heading or anything. He guessed they were happy scrambling up through the weather-hardened plants, getting away from the beach. Devil you knew, he figured. Didn't know what he would've told them if he'd had to justify it. Lost dads. Reincarnated feathered fathers. Hereditary water tamers.

Heh, what if he told them about the ocean talk.

Imagine that.

Crikey, the carnage.

Geez, he was even talking like dingo now.

But Witi hadn't heard his father's voice for a while and sensed he was about to be quizzed on where the hell they were heading. He leant against a tree and took in some deep breaths. Jordy squatted against the tree opposite while Alana held her hands behind her head.

Well? she asked.

A bit further I reckon, he said. He looked up the hill and saw the silhouette of his dad disappear behind a cluster of burly limestone rocks. They were the size of cars, protruding from the hillside like warts on someone's knuckles. Long strands of root the thickness of Koro's dreadlocks cradled the prehistoric faces while their leafy tops sat proudly above like toupees on a bunch of bald guys.

You guys see? Witi asked, still looking.

What's that? asked Jordy.

Nah, nothin'.

Between two of the boulders was a dark slit. They stood looking at blackness and the compressed dirt leading into it. Witi stepped to-wards the cave.

Witi, wait, Alana said. Shouldn't we ...

What's the worst, huh? Witi gave her a wink. It's my ancestral land. And anyway – he reached into his wetsuit and pulled out his mobile phone – I've got a torch.

The opening was hardly wider than his shoulders. It was dark inside, second darkest place he'd been that day.

He heard Alana. *You okay? Witi?*

The torchlight lit the whole area. Not a very big space but live-able. The dirt floor definitely looked disturbed, like something or someone had been here before them. He looked up at the ceiling and then the walls.

What the ... Hey, guys, you gotta see this.

Eyes like ocean currents

Eyes like glistening sand

Like tepid water

Like twin lows

Entwined, like the moon and sun

Pinned to blue skies threatening storms

On a sea of dead faces

The torch dimmed and the writing on the walls disappeared. Damn shit battery. Witi felt his heart pounding, loud as.

Who the hell would write that? asked Jordy, his Aussie tone reverberating. Specially here, in the middle of bumfark nowhere?

Witi's dad, that's who.

They cranked up Alana's phone next and they all read segments of writing. Jordy was the first to get sick of it.

Your old man wrote farkin' dribble, mate. No offence.

Alana stuck at it longer but Witi could tell that the novelty she'd experienced in the comfort of his bedroom was lost, probably washed from her in the river or blown away by the wind.

We're close though, huh? she said.

He's been here, he said. Mighta been the whole time.

Why would he? she said. He hiding? Or was he waiting?

Depends if you're talking to Mum or Koro.

Tomorrow might be the day, she said, moving back towards Jordy. Soon he could hear them talking gently in between roars from the wind outside.

Talking about me again, Witi thought. Most likely.

Just a soft murmur juxtaposed against the violent weather.

Probably thought he was as loony as his father.

Jordy didn't understand all this. He couldn't read

the flow

the rhythm

Couldn't read music when it was staring back at him.

But Witi could.

Fuckin' genius, Dad was.

Witi read all the walls, and when he'd finished he read the roof. Okay, so he didn't understand *all* of it, but most of it. One word stood out over the others:

Koro.

Not the word itself, but how he'd written it one particular time. The two o's were eyes with slanted lines above them and a sad smile below.

By the time Alana's battery died Witi had a new understanding of his father. As surreal as that was. He handed back the phone and apologised for using the remaining power.

Their eyes adjusted until they could see each other's silhouette. Sometimes the wind got so strong, the branches outside scraped their fingers on the entrance and each time the three of them would gape into the darkness, waiting to see if a black figure was gonna join them. When the noise stopped they'd look for comfort at each other.

Witi doubted he was showing as much white in his eyes as they were, but he was still kinda scared.

Not *scared*, scared, eh. Just scared of what his dad was gonna be like if he was still alive like Koro reckoned.

Would he be the same? Would he remember Witi? Would he be normal?

Would he still call him *pal*?

Mum said he wasn't well when he left.

He'd gone feral in their house, and back then he was *surrounded* by normality.

Jesus, what chance did he have of being normal *here*?

Living in the ground. Using charcoal to write across the walls and roof like a prisoner lamenting freedom. What did he eat? Where did he sleep? Witi's old man, the famous musician.

Now a wild man seeking refuge in the wilderness, but ...

But they'd finally found him where others couldn't.

Been here the whole time it turned out.

Probably been here while he was still with Mum and Witi, while he was walking around in his undies and writing in that diary of his. He was just waiting for his body to follow him. Yeah, mentally he'd been here all along.

Alana slid around to his side and rested her head on Witi's shoulder. He felt her breaths eventually deepen into sleep.

Saving the world, Koro reckoned. Didn't see no capes hanging up here, though. No utility belts. No shiny steel poles to slide down.

Would Witi still be his pal?

Thoughts like that went over and over in his mind.

Over and over.

Until somewhere along the line he fell asleep too.

SOMETHING GOING ON HERE

There was a high-pitched whirring. Witi opened his eyes.

He was still sitting with his back against the wall, aching. Alana had been using his lap as a pillow. Hearing the noise, she lifted her head. She looked at Witi and raised a hand to his forehead.

You're burning up, she said. You okay?

Shh, he whispered. You hear that?

Yeah, she said, but look at your hair. Your face. You're saturated.

Nah, sweet, he said, giving her his best Richie McCaw. He didn't have the energy to explain things to her. It could wait. Truth was, he was just stoked someone else could finally hear something he could.

The sound was riding the wind and bouncing off the cave walls so they couldn't tell whether it was getting further away or had parked itself outside the entrance. It definitely wasn't cyclone-related.

Jordy was already up, clinging to the wall near the opening with just his head outside.

It's a drone, he said.

Alana scrambled to her feet. They're looking for us!

Jordy fended her back. She tried to wrestle past but he had her blocked, a few years of Aussie Rules or league or whatever dingos do coming into play.

Whaddya doing? Let me out. We've gotta let them know where we are.

Jordy shook his head. It's not looking for us, he said. He peered back outside. It's looking for me.

It's *what*?

Jordy looked at Alana, then at Witi, finishing somewhere between them like the answer was written in the air. But any words he might've said were lost with the buzz of the drone sailing past the entrance, close enough to blacken the light momentarily. Jordy followed its flight path, motioning with one of his big mitts for the other two to stay put.

Witi doubted Alana knew about his past, the scenes of tubes, tits and fists.

Doubt she'd give a toss anyway, Witi reckoned, because he sure as hell wouldn't have wanted to be on the end of the shove she gave Jordy's chest.

Hey, what the fark?

She shoved him hard into the limestone wall. Who are they?

Awright, he said holding his palms out. Quit with the feistiness. It's my dad, or some of his team. They're not really here for me. More like the same reason we're here, kind of. Same waves, different intent. Gonna be a little hard to explain.

Witi stepped closer.

Don't really know what to say, Jordy continued. My dad's not really in the climate change business. More like the energy business. He get's employed by a company, group, could be your own government for all I know, to ... to prospect.

Like oil prospecting? Why would they wanna do that during a damn cyclone? Witi asked.

Nah, Jordy said. Nah, different. Something I suspect the oil barons of the world would pay big money to make ... you know, disappear. That map I showed you, the one with the reef formations? There's something going on here they want.

Yeah? Witi said. Like what? Stand-up barrels, I s'pose? He laughed and nudged Alana with his elbow. But Jordy was right, she was fired up. No wink gonna save dingo now.

Like what? she demanded. What could they possibly want with a beach?

Jordy let out a sigh. Not the beach, he said, the waves. Geez, don't you listen?

He leant back against the wall and his face was dissected vertically by black shadow.

Look, he continued, I don't know ... honestly, I don't. Everything's been such a farkin' secret in the old man's life. You've got no idea what he's like. I was just stoked he finally asked me to be involved. But my only job was to get you here. That's it, swear to God.

Witi scoffed. Get me here? You set me up? You set us *both* up? The whole time?

The old man had your name. I just had to find out a bit about you. To make sure, you know—that whatever info he had on you and your family was true.

Now who's full of shit, Witi said. So that fight on the first day, you must've ...

I was looking for a reason to get in your good books. Man, that couldn't have been scripted better.

And at our house, that's why you snooped ...

Actually, I thought it was harmless – I just had to make sure you were the real deal. Had no idea it was gonna lead to anything.

Yet here we are, said Alana.

To be fair, Witi's pop did a better job than me. Something is important about this place, important enough to send us here. The people who pay my father have some serious coinage behind them. Did ya see the precision of that drone? That didn't come from your local Harvey Norman. It's flying around in a cyclone. Nah, that's A-grade military tech right there. Bet the cops here don't even know something that stealth is in the country.

We should go and see him anyway, Alana said. He can take us home, then get on with whatever he wants to do. Doesn't worry me what he's up to.

You don't know my old man.

I know he didn't walk here like we did.

It ain't that easy.

Surely ...

It ain't.

Alana walked towards the light anyway. She'd never let a tourist tell her what to do. But Jordy grabbed her arm.

They'll hurt you if you go out there, he said.

That's just stupid. She tried to shake her arm free. But he had her in his vice of fingers. He leant in close.

You have to trust me on this, he said. It's all a set-up.

Let me go! Alana shoved her free forearm under Jordy's throat and pinned him to the wall. He didn't struggle, and even though his eyes were soon red and glazed he also wasn't afraid. But he wasn't letting go of Alana.

Through gritted teeth he said to Witi: They don't care about her, but they will hurt her to get to you, mate. *They want you*, Witi. Just like they wanted your father eight years ago.

Wait, what? Witi said. Alana, let him go.

She gave Jordy one last push then stepped back. Jordy let go too, and rubbed his throat.

Touch me like that again and you'll be a lot more sorry, she said. Asshole.

I'm really sorry, guys, Jordy said. I was just trying to please my old man.

Witi looked at the writing on the walls:

Hold everyone to ransom. A new cornerstone.

Who has the most energy wins, sits on the power throne.

At any expense can't let paradise reside.

Kiss that goodbye

wants are never satisfied

And he thought about the stuff Koro had told him about protecting the environment from others. Was Jordy's dad the one he was talking about? What were they capable of?

I think he's right, Witi said. Babe, you gotta leave.

Don't you mean we? She waved a finger between them both. As in, we have to go?

Nah, Witi replied. I think I gotta stay.

You're not serious? I can't get out on my own.

There's something I have to do. Something important.

Witi, what the hell?

SIT ON THE POWER THRONE

For the first time Witi felt cold, like cold was growing from inside his bones. So, hungry too. Re-reading the walls wasn't helping either:

> *Stand in the ocean*
> *And feel another world*
> *A wave speaks to you*
> *And the door motions*
> *That's when we protect and shut it again*
> *To fix what's broken*
> *Before the blackness spills*
> *And your destiny is spoken*

Jordy was sitting upright and giving Alana major stink-eye. She stood leaning against the entrance, staring westward. Probably thinking about her parents and how they'd be asking the overworked emergency services to help look for their only daughter. She turned back to Jordy with a blacker look than he'd ever seen on her.

Whaddya waiting for? Jordy finally said. You heard Witi – it's actually best you get going.

Just how dangerous are we talking here? she asked.

You don't wanna know. Then again, I reckon your aggro would work in nicely with Dad's squad goals.

With that remark, he raised his hands in submission, sarcastically of course. She ignored him and searched the hills for a clear path.

Why didn't you tell me earlier? Witi asked. That time back at my house, you could've said something.

You don't get it. I knew about you all along. Why do you think I ended up at your college? I was sent to ... I was there to research you. Because your dad and my dad have a history. That room in your house just confirmed it all.

Where's my dad? What happened to him?

Dunno, man, I was the same age as you when he shot the gap.

But you said ...

I know what I said. They would've been looking for your dad 'cos he was obviously the Aquarian guy 'round here. And before you start, I dunno what an Aquarian is, only every time my old man gets sent to the next elusive Spot X there's some guy he and his team of science boffins call an Aquarian. It's not even a real word, just nerd speak. But it turns out no one's seen your old man, number one on the Aquarian hit list, but they know all about his one-son offspring and you're the next big thing on their agenda.

What, me?

Ta farkin' daa.

Witi was stuck trying to process the information, wondering what personal crap he'd gifted this guy.

Alana asked if he'd been to more places than just Australia.

Nah, not me. This is the first time Dad's wanted me to do any-thing. Actual. But I know he's visited places like Hawaii, Mexico. Portugal. A few other coastal spots. There's a heap of unexplored coast in the world. Surfers don't have the resources like the groups my old man works for has. They have the world's surf breaks, known and unknown, at their fingertips. Except to them they represent something polar opposite to what the waxhead population is after.

Prospecting.

Yeah, that's right.

For energy.

Shitloads of it.

To do what with?

Your dad says it up there. To sit on the power throne. Hold the world to ransom.

You'd betray them too? Alana asked. Or are we the only stupid ones to fall for it in the first place?

Believe it or not, he said, this was the safest option.

Alana raised a sudden finger to her lips. Voices, she whispered. Someone's out there.

They stared at each other. No one moved. They heard the yelling clear as, like commands, but not the words.

We need to get out of here, Jordy said.

To where? There's nowhere else to go, she replied. Anyway, what if you're just gonna lead us to them?

They'll find us in here, and we'll be trapped, said Jordy. We'd better head for higher ground and quick before they get closer. It's your choice whether to believe me or not.

They scratched their way through the bracken, holding the trunks of scarred gorse to haul themselves up. The neoprene barrier of their wetsuits saved them from cuts. While none of them spoke there was plenty of noise from rolling debris they kicked loose and shaking vegetation. The wind hadn't stopped but the rain had and in Witi's mind that was just as sweet. With no food or water, and no sense of safety, they soon grew exhausted. At one point Alana slipped. Her arms waved like slow-motion windmills to suspend gravity's grip, just long enough for Jordy to reach out and grab her waist, pulling her to safety.

She pushed his hand away and stepped ahead of him.

At the top they hid behind hefty rocks and peered back down into the cove. The swell had risen overnight and where they'd surfed the day before, the waves now defied the possible on this coast. Giant chasms of water rushed towards the beach, exploding with enough power for them to feel the vibrations through the rocks they were leaning on. Witi felt a surge of despair. These were the biggest waves he'd seen by a long shot. Thing was, he had seen them before:

in the darkness of night.

in the heat of his sleep.

He had ridden them,

surfed them

and been struck down into the darkness,

the darkness of the night

where Koro said his wairua had shown him.

He didn't see the two men down on the shore with guns slung on their bodies until Jordy mentioned it.

That's why ya can't just waltz on down there, he whispered.

Why all the armour? Witi asked. Bit serious ain't it?

The world's at an energy crux, it's a war out there. Industrial espionage, man – heard of that? They don't wanna take chances.

They watched the two black figures roam the beach, looking at the area. They stumbled in the wind but seemed unfazed. A double-bladed helicopter glided into view around the headland, carrying what looked like a shipping container. It landed the container as a second chopper appeared and did the same. More soldier-type figures spilled out of the chopper doors and ran from the rotors as the machines rose again, leaving the containers on the beach. The soldiers got busy, some securing the containers to the ground while others opened them and started moving new technical equipment in smaller boxes. A couple of seals waddled up to check them out. Maybe the soldiers were getting too close to their pups. Light flashed off the barrel of one rifle before the crackle of automatic gunfire reached them. There was enough force in the bullets to roll the seals back across the sand in a trail of red.

What are they doing? Alana was in disbelief. She slid off the rock and faced away.

Jordy was looking at Witi: here was proof of how dangerous his dad's little secret team were. Seriously, there was almost a smirk on his face like he was stoked he'd been vindicated. Then again, these were his breed. Maybe he was enjoying the show. Secretly wishing he had a gun to shoot up the wildlife, make him feel like the man too.

The other seals have done a runner, he said. They're outta danger.

Witi expected Alana to resume her place between them, but the air remained cold. Instead he heard her say his name.

Witi.

Witi.

He turned to see two men standing just outside the edge of the bush in black military uniforms, their faces hidden in balaclavas. They were staring along the scopes of their high-powered rifles that pointed directly at them. One raised a hand to his ear and started communicating with someone.

Witi slowly pulled Alana to her feet and put her between him and the rock. One of those guns could probably send a bullet through him and her in an instant, but there was a chance he could shield her, even just to slow it down.

Farkin'ell! Jordy yelled. C'mon, you guys. Really? Put the farkin' guns down. We haven't eaten for a couple of days, we're tired and thirsty—you really think we need a coupla barrels to keep us in check? Put them down.

Your father wants you and the boy back at the chopper, one of them yelled in a deep, gravel voice, loud enough to be heard over the sound of the gale around them.

Probably spent a life in combat situations shouting over bombs and shit so his throat was worn like sandpaper and that was just the way he talked now.

You, the soldier said. Girl, you're free to go. He motioned with the muzzle for her to leave.

Witi felt her hands tighten around his hips.

Go, he repeated.

Witi moved quietly aside to let her pass. It's for the best, he said.

Witi, I can't ...

Head west. Just keep running, you'll be safe.

What if these guys hurt you? What if I get lost and can't get help in time?

Witi saw the fantail swoop behind the soldiers and into the thick vegetation. Follow the bird, he told her. It led you before, didn't it?

Move! the soldier yelled.

Witi saw the intensity in Alana's eyes. She kissed his cheek. This might be the best day of his life.

Run, he whispered.

She did, but before the trees consumed her she turned for one last look. Witi gave her a subtle thumbs-up and then she was gone.

Jordy took a step forward, then another. His hands were semi raised. C'mon guys, he said, drop the guns.

They didn't.

Jordy continued, and the barrels didn't move from Witi.

Stand down, Jordy! one of them said.

But Jordy's foot moved forward, then his other.

You're not gonna shoot him, you idiots, Jordy said. The old man would never allow it. He *needs* him to finish the job.

The other soldier suddenly swung his barrel at Jordy, so close Jordy must've felt the cold steel on his forehead. You're not authorised to give orders, the man said.

Jordy stood still.

Between the rumble of the waves at Witi's back and the offshore wind screaming in his face and the thought of his ancestors guiding Alana, he heard his name called and saw his father standing down the ridgeline from them, perfectly framed in a swaying canopy of fern.

Witi must've looked like he'd seen a ghost because one soldier turned, following his gaze. The other did too. And Jordy made his move.

Drew on his skills from league or Aussie Rules or whatever dingos do and tackled them both.

Guns, utility belts, black lace-up boots, bulletproof vests and everything, all tangled up in Jordy and his wetsuit.

One big driving tackle.

They didn't see it comin'.

Run! Jordy yelled. Go!

So Witi did.

He leapt and scrambled to where his dad was.

Where he'd been, 'cos he wasn't there anymore.

Stop! a soldier called out behind him like he was yelling over bombs and shit.

But Witi didn't stop.

Fastest goofy feet in the land that day.

They must've been pissed 'cos he heard the crack of gunfire.

Just one shot.

Maybe a warning shot,

maybe aiming directly at him,

maybe a misfire.

But it happened just as he dived head first into the safety of the native trees and bushes whose mauri once nurtured his ancestors.

He picked himself up, and as he ran blindly through random branches and thick bracken he couldn't help but wonder where that bullet actually ended up.

CYAN AND YELLOW-WHITE

Witi was in blackness, like normal. Except ...

There was no sudden awakening. No sitting up in a bed. No sweats.

Just voices here, there. Whispers everywhere.

And someone began pushing him from below and pulling from above like a hundred fantails were making him fly. And as he rose, the blackness was being diluted with various shades of grey and light.

He couldn't make out what was being said, but he thought of his mum sitting at the end of his bed and the soft words she'd use to see if he was asleep or when she wanted him awake. And he thought of her trapped at the kitchen table, staring across at her dad who'd pushed the love of her life away, then her only son. And he watched her bury her face in her arms and weep, and he felt the snap of her heart as it broke.

Tears washing across his face
in a symphony of voices
and a blaze of light.

He opened his eyes.

The incoming tide was slapping at his face.

Somewhere in his escape he must've slipped and fallen down a ravine.

Knocked himself out, eh.

He only knew this because he was bent like a plastic twisty toy amongst boulders and his head hurt like hell. And there was a broken branch in his fist from the wounded tree overhanging twenty metres above him.

There was a river at the bottom of the gully. Might've been the same one he and Jordy had caught a ride on; it had the same frenzied flow and the same silt-brown colour. It joined the ocean like chaos and confusion meeting. The river's raging torrent threw logs at the sea, but its salt-water sibling simply picked them up in its shore break and biffed them up on the beach with the others. Thunder and white noise. And quiet whispers. To him at least.

He eased himself up on one elbow and checked whether his head was still functional:

what day it was,

why he was here,

why he was *really* here,

all that sorta stuff.

Stuff he couldn't answer anyway.

He watched as a drowned rimu trunk appeared from the depths offshore and started rolling in slow motion up the beach towards him. It would take a sizeable machine to move a log like that, but right now it was bounding up the rocks like it was a twig. He scrambled backwards, searching for grip on the slippery boulders, trying for higher ground, but the cliff face stopped him and he watched helplessly as the trunk crashed and moaned its way closer. Its jagged branches splintered on the boulders, turning the whole mass into something resembling a giant medieval torture device.

The tide was pushing it right at him. An extra big surge. Yeah, just his luck.

He covered his head in his arms and tucked his feet in.

He braced himself and squeezed and felt the trunk's massive shadow blacken the air and he wondered:

what part of him was gonna be impaled?

And how days later they'd find his rotted body spiked to this thing like a giant shish kebab and they'd say,

Man, who the hell deserved to go like that?

And he also imagined he was sitting on a secluded beach staring at perfect six-foot Fijian wave, with only a lone coconut tree above and the turquoise shimmer of water. And Alana, laughing at something witty he'd just said and afterwards she and her dimples nestled into his shoulder and as he dipped his hat over his brow she gently fingered the strings on his guitar and asked:

Man, what would you give to stay here forever?

Witi threw his hands out, like he was stopping traffic.

No! he yelled until his lungs felt like they'd imploded.

His eyes were still closed, still waiting for the sensation of wood making its first ugly puncture through his skin.

He opened them when he sensed the light had returned. The whispers had stopped.

The log was retreating with the water. He stood and followed it towards the ocean, like he was shepherding it away. Any normal person would've taken the opportunity to get the hell out of there. But he guessed he wasn't normal, doubted he ever had been.

Yeah, nah, guess he wanted to know for certain, eh.

Apparently he'd stopped a river once.

When he stepped into the frenzied water the ocean formed a perfect dry circle around his ankle. It did the same with his other foot too. Soon he'd pushed the log twenty metres offshore beyond the low-tide mark, and where he should've been swept out to his death with it he was standing in a cylinder of dryness as the waves broke everywhere around him, but never on him.

Felt like he was in the centre of the world. Or the world was centring on him.

He couldn't comprehend it, but he was doing it. He shut his eyes; maybe he'd find himself sitting back on the beach, back at the cave, or back at home cleaning the shed. Sitting on the bed with Alana. Standing with his dad's guitar poised over his shoulder, ready to munt the hell out of it on some dude's head. He hoped for all of the above. But when he opened his eyes again, all he got was the centre of the world.

With a hive of voices again, and kahawai that swam up to him and flashed their silver as they fled in fear when they realised there was nothing webbed about him. But that wasn't the strangest thing.

When he touched the sea walls sparks of energy flew from his fingers, electric sparks of cyan and yellow-white. His fingers tingled with the sensation and when he ran them up and down the water the voices changed — highs and lows and a range of keys like synchronised wind chimes, depending on where he placed them. And the walls grew higher when he hooked his fingers into each side and raised his hands. Man, the sound of that was like an evangelistic church choir.

He was so swept up with the sensation, he took a while to notice the dark shadow coming towards him through the water. Moving like it had arms and legs, like someone was walking under the water as naturally as if they were in the park. Yeah, he knew that silhouette.

His dad stood eye to eye with him just on the outside of the dry and smiled.

He hadn't aged. He was exactly how Witi remembered him, eh. Exactly.

Witi went to throw his arms around him but he felt only cold water. His dad's face and body broke into dozens of ripples, as if he were trying to rub out his own reflection in a pond. Witi thrashed at the water seeking the sensation of human flesh. The sound and sparks were intense. But his dad's image never moved; he just waited for things to settle and for Witi to see that he was staring and pointing back to land.

Witi eventually gave in and nodded. But he didn't want to leave. He held his hand to the liquid surface, barely touching, but enough to feel the tingle. His dad raised his own and placed his palm against his son's.

In the next surge of debris and disturbed sea floor, Witi watched his dad fade away.

WITH EVERY INHALE

There was nowhere to go but back up the river and into the ravine, where his dad had pointed. He should've been buzzing out, full of adrenaline. He'd just walked out of the ocean dry. But he'd also come face to face with his lost father and hadn't shared a word. Hadn't heard his warm earthy voice. Not felt a ruffle of the hair like he remembered. Not even the sensation of a father's solid hand on his son's shoulder. He'd done no more than come face to face with a memory, a life-sized photo straight from his adolescence. Jesus, did Witi still look ten years younger to his dad?

Even sticking one foot in front of the other was a mission, especially over the rocks and logs and through the wind that rushed up the channel.

Witi leant down and drank from the river, then stood and spat out the specks of dirt and wondered if he could even risk wasting energy on a further dodgy walk.

Coulda killed for a cheese and Marmite sandwich 'bout now.

From behind the sound of thrashing water came the buzzing of a drone in flight. He saw it drift sideways in the air above the river mouth and stop mid-flight as it seemed to stare at him. Who was controlling it, and from where? This close he could make out two barrels like the rifles the soldiers had pointed at him. Jordy was right, the drone was military grade and if this had been anywhere else, completely badass. But he'd seen enough sci-fi movies to know what happened next. As he turned and started to run up the valley, the familiar ring of an Australian's voice came over a loud speaker. It came from the drone.

Wait, Witi. We're gonna land and we can talk. They have food.

Yeah, nah.

He ran.

He heard the drone's rotors rev up to follow, but the ravine's walls moved closer and the trees and vegetation reached together to form a canopy that even its high-tech navigation found hard to manoeuvre through. As Witi made ground away from it he could still hear Jordy's plea over the speaker:

Gimme a chance ...

safe ...

find her ...

do it together ...

That sorta stuff.

When he thought he was in far enough up the river he stopped under a tree. From the safety of its thick trunk, he watched through its foliage as the large black shape headed away. He collapsed back onto the earth of the riverbank and stared up at nothing. He listened to make sure the drone had left. When he was certain, he let his breathing loose and swore that the mauri from his ancestors must've entered him with every inhale.

He laughed. Well, it started out as a laugh.

When he turned his head and felt the grit move under his scalp and tried to focus on the fantail on the ground a couple of feet away dancing with itself

well, he felt nothing but raw hopelessness.

Hey, little fullah, he said gulping deeply, haven't seen a beautiful girl by any chance? Think you'd know her if ya did. Beautiful.

Don't talk, huh? Figures, you're just a bird.

Just thought, you know.

Guess I hoped.

Don't matter.

Heh.

Of course it *did* understand him, though.

This one wanted him to climb the cliff. It flicked from rata vine to rata vine, up, then down, then up some more. Whoever was in charge of that drone knew where he'd gone, where he'd be, so he couldn't exactly hang around. Maybe this fantail had come across a beautiful girl after all.

So he started climbing the strong vines like he was a superhero scaling a building.

Feeding on what little adrenaline remained.

About halfway up the fantail vanished. One moment within a weak arm's reach, then gone. Looking for movement he saw only crumbling lumps of dirt falling from his bare toes as they scratched into the cliff face. When they hit the ground they exploded. Maybe he'd better cut his losses and head down and think of a Plan B. But when he looked up again, the bird was back.

Where'd you go?

Nah, nuthin'.

His answer lay in the next lift, the next step, the next strain. Another cave. But this one was smaller, just enough for one person from what he could see as he struggled to pull himself up onto the ledge. The fantail flew away and he was left alone halfway up some random cliff face in the middle of some energy coup being played out on his ancestral land. But that wasn't entirely true.

When his eyes adjusted to the dark he discovered he wasn't alone at all.

DARK SOCKETS

He'd never seen a dead body before – not a real one, anyway. And if he had, he'd imagine it'd look like the person did before they were dead, just paler and stiffer. Not like the version slumped in the corner of the cave in a foetal position, all bone and dust. Arms resting together at the chest like they'd been cold, or feeling for the last beats of their heart.

Dark sockets stared at him from its tilted head.

And he stared back.

He must've done this in silence for a while, until he became aware of voices from the soldiers far below. He scrambled further into the cave. He sat with his back against the wall next to the skeleton.

And together they stared outside at the light.

Soon all he could hear was his breathing. From the corners of his eyes he looked at the skull.

So this was what his old man had spoken about. Ancestors buried in caves and all that.

Witi should've been more freaked out, fleeing the place out of respect. But he was weak. Reckoned he was getting a little delusional by now too. But that wasn't it, really.

His ancestral land, eh. He was sitting next to his own flesh and blood. Well, bone anyway. Told himself no harm could come from that.

He looked around the cave, his eyes adjusted by now. Not much of a burial site. Just a dirty hole in the side of a cliff.

No ancient relics.

No burial robe.

No markings on the wall.

Except ...

He leant over and brushed away a cobweb, then wiped the dust too. He gave it a final blow for good measure. He took a closer look then reeled back.

Suddenly he *was* freaked:

<pre>
            8003008 8003008 80
         8003008 8003008 8003008 800
        0880030088003008   3008 8
        00880030088003008   00300
       300880030088003008   8
       0300880030088003 0088
      80030088003008pal800300800
      888003008800300880030088 0038003
     00880300880030088003008800 300880030
     8003008 8003008 8003008 8003008 8003008 8003
   8003008 8003008 8003008 8003008 80030088 003008 800300
 8003008 8003008 8003008 8003008 8003008 8003008 8003008 8003
8003008 8003008 8003008 8003008 8003008 8003008 8003008 8003008
8003008 8003008 8003008 8003008 8003008 8003008 8003008 8003008 800
</pre>

Dad? That you?

But they just stared at each other.

Jesus, he said, what happened?

And waited for an answer.

Mighta been a few seconds or maybe a few minutes, he didn't know, but Witi had an overwhelming urge to touch the skeleton. He wanted to connect in some way, just to feel what wairua was left.

But the closer he leant, the more he saw ...

there was an ancient relic.

The edge of a taiaha buried under dust and pointing away from the body.

A burial robe. Well, some sort of material that had been plaited and decorated with feathers and leathery-looking stuff. It must've been pretty cool-looking at the time and acted as a wrap to keep the body in its sitting position. But time had worn holes and degraded its strength and he could see where bones had broken through. Nah, no way this was his dad.

He got closer still.

His breath disturbing fine dust.

And in the faint light he saw the tip of something inside its hands. It wasn't grasping for a heart, but holding something to it. Underneath was string in a tight coil. He reached in and pinched it between his thumb and forefinger, and pulled it free. The string unravelled as he did so.

He held it up and stared at the polished bone dangling in front of his eyes.

The same polished whale-bone.

Shaped in the same style as ... yeah.

He pulled his own necklace free and held it alongside. When he brought the two pieces together they locked perfectly into place, as his father had shown him all those years ago. A new weight grew in his hands, like something was now inside it. He hung it around his neck with his own.

He fell in the foetal position himself, and held the carving tight in his fist.

Too exhausted to do anything else.

Too emotionally drained to give any fucks.

His head still hurt like hell.

But he was relieved to know that this wasn't the old man. Convinced himself of that much. His dad wore jeans for all occasions, not formal burial attire a few hundred years old.

He'd been here, though. And Witi reckoned he'd known his son'd visit soon enough. Shoved the other half in the hand of an ancestor to hand on to him.

Bet he cracked a bit of a smile with that little creative touch. Witi slid back to the other side of the cave and imagined his dad being here, waiting for him. Sitting in the darkness, staring out at the only circle of light. Waiting to see if this all had a point. Whether his son would turn up. Guess he got sick of that.

Witi must've cried himself to sleep because when he woke, the sun was shining directly into the cave and his eyes were itchy-as.

He sat up.

His head felt better, though.

His whole body felt ready, like he'd just eaten a massive bowl of Weet-Bix or a double-decker Marmite and cheese sandwich.

Weirdest feeling, eh.

His fist was pulsing where it held the carving, as if small surges of energy were being pumped into him. Feeding him.

He tucked it inside his wetsuit and felt it sync with his heartbeat. What distant member of the whānau had he just met, just shared a cave with? And if his dad hadn't given him the other half of the pendant all those years ago, would he still be here?

Right now he was feeling great.

Could this thing do that?

He had to get back to his mum.

He had to find Alana.

Had to speak to Koro.

But mostly, he had to see Mum again.

Man, she'd be havin' kittens.

MYTHS AND LIES

The climb out of the cave was way easier than the climb in.

On a small ledge near the top of the cliff he stopped, bracing himself with each gust. From up here he could see far out to the ocean horizon; the cyclone was moving and with it the wind had now swung to howl from offshore. There were parallel lines of clean groundswell all the way to the sky. Rolling to shore in perfect unison – never faster than the one in front, never slower than the one behind. In this battle of Earth's elements, the ocean swell and the gale-force winds collided to form titanic poetry. Each one could have been a carbon copy of the other, anyone else would've seen it like that. But he didn't.

To him each wave was as unique as a fingerprint.

Each wave had its own wairua.

Its own personality.

These watery giants with white manes of hairspray trailing in the offshore wind. From up here, it might've seemed only a four-foot swell, but he saw a large flock of seagulls, high in the air and blown chaotically in the wind, disappear into the troughs between waves.

Each wave ate the headland rock like it was bite-sized.

And each one spoke to him in a tone so deep its voice vibrated through the rata vine he was holding.

Once he'd reached the top he started running inland. But still the voices came, from every tree, leaf, every ripple within a puddle. In the end he lost all bearings and didn't know where he was going. He was just runnin'.

Must've been ages before he finally stopped. He recognised the area he was moving through, with the craggy limestone outcrop. He quietened his goofy feet through the undergrowth as he slowed to a creep.

Dingo knew where their cave was, eh.

He would've told those soldier boys to stake the joint out. Just in case Witi came back.

Or Alana.

Witi crept up a rock face. He crawled to the edge and from under the cover of kuripaka fronds he watched the cave entrance directly below. He stayed for ages just looking and listening. But the only evidence that Jordy's mates had been there were boot marks in the dirt at the entrance. He was about to jump down when the black muzzle of a rifle emerged into the daylight. He fell flat to his stomach again. The metal stayed where it was – hovered in the air like a snake's head – then retracted into the darkness beneath him.

He back-tracked carefully, feet-first, until the familiar sensation of wet vegetation was between his toes. He exhaled slowly.

A hand wrapped itself around Witi's mouth. Before he could wrench an opening he was being dragged backwards. All he could do was stare up at the fantail doing loop-the-loops amongst the canopy like it had something happy to say.

Quiet, lad, a voice whispered. *We gotcha.*

When the hands released him he turned to see a face smiling back, the wrinkles wrapping around the corners of his eyes like lines of swell on a point break.

Koro!

He clapped a hand back onto Witi's gob.

Shhh, lad, don't want any attention. No good dodging bullets at my age, eh.

Witi swung his arms around him and felt Koro's heavy palm settle on his back.

We gotcha, he repeated.

Witi stepped back. We? he said. Who else is here?

But Koro wasn't even looking at him.

His smile had been replaced by a look of curiosity. Eventually Witi saw the waves on his face begin wrapping again.

You found him, didn't you, Koro said, still not making eye contact. You found ya old man. Thank Zion, we're saved.

But Witi had had enough of his ramblings. Koro, who else?

Koro motioned with his head and there was Witi's mum's outlined in the shadows. Had to be her because her smile stood out like a full moon. Her hands were urging him to her and suddenly they were back home and he was a four-year-old with a red welt across his cheek after Dad's guitar string broke while he was playing it, and he was in desperate need of a hug. Now there was his mum down on one knee and beaming him into her bosom. Through the pain and over her shoulder he suddenly saw his dad crossed-legged on the floor, playing with five strings and singing quietly some song that must've been popular 'cos Mum joined in with him and they were so beautiful together it could dry tears.

Sorry, Mum, I should never ...

It's okay, son, she said softly. We got you now.

Witi had so many questions and things to tell he didn't know where to start or even if he could without tripping over himself. Some things could wait until they were back in their normal house, sitting in their normal chairs around their normal table, with a plate of sandwiches so big it was anything but normal. Other things couldn't.

You seen Alana? he asked.

She shook her head, perplexed.

Why would ... no, she said. Why would we?

And for the first time he noticed the dirt on her face and the debris in her hair, evidence of her effort to get here. All of which did nothing to soften her expression when her face turned to thunder as she realised that this was even more than a one-son hunt.

She was running back, he said. Thought you guys mighta, you know ...

I was going to say something, lass, Koro pitched in, still whispering though higher pitched. But you were in such a hurry to leave to find the lad.

Her too? And you let this happen? You should've stayed on the coast to let the storm deal to you. Heaven knows it's the one thing as big as your insanity.

They said that about your man once.

He was *sick*, you old fool. I brought him home so you could fix him. Instead you made him that way.

Koro folded his arms high on his chest. I opened his eyes to his destiny, he said. That man of yours was here to save us. He did his job. You knew that. You know it still.

You filled his head with myths and lies.

He was special.

Mum huffed. Well, at least we agree on that much, she said.

Really? Witi interrupted. You guys doing this here? Now?

She turned back to her son and held his head between her palms and looked so deep into his eyes he thought she was gonna fall in.

C'mon, son, let's see if we can find her on the way home.

But Witi felt Koro grip his arm and pull him back.

He can't go yet, he said. Lad's got a job to do.

Take your hand off him, she said, yanking Witi towards her. Jesus, I hope you find what you're looking for.

I already have, he said, and so has Witi. See?

He pointed at a faint blue light throbbing through the neoprene on Witi's chest.

Witi reckoned he must've looked as surprised as his mum to see it. It was like his heart was a stage light

Show her, lad, he said. That necklace you got in there.

Witi pulled it out and it cast the three of them into its blue glow. Koro was grinning, the sapphire falling through the gaps in his teeth.

Is he …? Did you …? His mum suddenly wasn't sure how to ask the most important questions.

I dunno, Mum, I've seen a skeleton … but don't worry, it wasn't him, I was led to it – stumbled across it by accident. Like, this thing is ages old. In a cave. Not far from here. I could, you know, take you if you want, but heh, you know, it's sacred and tapu to do that, so yeah. Anyway, I found this there. Think Dad wanted me to find it.

But his mum raised a hand, so he stopped. She looked lost, as if she hardly knew where to put herself. Exhaustion overtook her, Koro and Witi lunging to catch her as her eyes rolled back and her knees buckled. Witi thought he saw his dad's hands there too, a frantic, unsuccessful grab with his ghost fingers.

PART IV

IN WATERY LIMBO

It didn't take her long to come to. When she did, she pushed herself back against the tree. Witi sat beside her and she reached for his hand.

He's still with me, Mum, he whispered. With us. Has been through everything. Nothing's changed, really.

She went to say something, but closed her mouth and smiled instead and squeezed his hand tightly. She held the necklace up and studied it. Witi had put it around her neck as she lay passed out. Already her skin was returning to its usual warm brown.

You hearing that, lad? That rumbling noise?

He did, but he'd become so accustomed to strange sounds it hadn't stood out.

Koro stood and reached to pull her to her feet. Help me out, lad, we need to keep moving.

Only place we're going is home, Mum said.

They heard a voice giving orders. It didn't sound far away.

We have no choice, Koro said, we have to leave this place, now. Those guys with guns are everywhere on this cove.

They might be looking for us, she said.

No, Mum, not in a good way, Witi said, lifting her to her feet. This time Koro's right. He's been right the whole time. We have to go.

They started running, while Witi searched frantically for the sign of his old man to guide them. A fantail to follow. A rata arrow. Anything. But this time he was on his own. Except for Koro ...

This way, Koro yelled.

Witi figured this was Koro's old stomping ground, his ancestral home, eh, figured he'd know the place well. He might've been old but after decades of exploring this land for wild pigs and other game he knew where to stand. He seemed happy when they reached a small creek.

I know where this goes, he said.

Witi alerted his mum to the change of direction and headed into the vegetation where Koro had disappeared. They sliced through branches and stepped out onto a large limestone outcrop high above the beach. Koro's open arms were barriers to keep them from toppling over the ledge – as the creek was doing – to the rock and sand below.

Witi felt like they were standing on the last piece of land in existence.

The wind trying to push them closer to the ledge.

Like the end had finally come.

It was being delivered by the fury of the ocean.

And it was the most beautiful thing he'd ever seen. Satin lines of rolling pulses.

In sets of six and seven and stacked to the furthest edge of the horizon.

Each set slightly bigger than the last.

Angrier looking.

More intimidating.

Shoulda been freaking out,

like his mum was, cowering behind Koro with two handfuls of his bush shirt. No good with heights, eh. He never knew.

But these lines of groundswell were so, so perfect. Super perfect.

He was a moth seeing his first-ever porch light.

He coulda stepped off the ledge to touch them.

Witi felt Koro tug him back, anchoring him to terra firma.

Easy there, lad.

Witi's body tingled with every wave that broke. Like sparks ignited. And it wasn't just his name being whispered this time – he heard it in every bone in his body, a noise like an orchestra doing a pre-gig tune-up.

It was so distracting he didn't hear the pair of drones rise from directly below them, like a mechanical whales breaching. Koro put his barriers out again and retreated, pushing them backwards.

Move, he yelled over the noise and wind.

Stop there! the voice from the drone's loudspeaker yelled.

Witi's mum let out a shriek like she'd seen a cockroach in the bathroom.

Four soldiers stepped out of the bush, pointing rifles at them.

They'd tracked them down the creek. And now they had them trapped on the rock with nowhere to go.

Witi looked back down the cliff, but saw no ledges, no handy vegetation to shimmy down. And even the best rugby-heads at school couldn't weave their way past the trigger-happy quartet in front of them. Their luck had run out and they were running on empty. But...

But yeah ...

Witi looked at the creek beside them and rubbed his tingling fingers in and out, making fists, not sure if he could do it.

He looked back at Koro, who nodded to Witi, like he knew. Of course he knew.

Get the boy! Quick! Witi heard.

Two of the soldiers stepped closer. Witi turned to the water, the tiny stream that it was, and closed his eyes. He made his hands into two large scoops and lifted them, feeling the sudden weight in his biceps. When he looked again, the stream was flowing through the air at shoulder height.

Witi! Mum screamed.

One of the soldiers raised his rifle. Witi twisted and pushed in his direction.

Water drove into both soldiers, knocking them off their feet. They skidded along the ground and into a boulder. Another soldier took aim at Witi. He pulled the trigger and the sound of a crack rang out. Witi raised an arm, expecting the force of the impact to blow him straight off the cliff. Instead, a shield of liquid flew up between them and the soldiers. Koro reached two fingers into the liquid and pinched out the bullet from its watery limbo.

He held it up and taunted them with it.

The third soldier let loose with a series of shots, each bullet stopping short of Koro's face. Witi threw his hands towards the soldier and two lines of hard water latched onto his shoulders. His rifle dropped to the ground as Witi lifted and manoeuvred him high onto the nearest tree branch. The remaining soldier stared at them from behind his black-tinted goggles. He had a firm grip on his gun but there was uncertainty in his stance. Witi stood prepared, hands out to the sides, kinda like he was going to tackle him if the soldier ran at him. They stared at one another as the wind whipped up a thin mist around them. Suddenly the barrel pointed upwards. Witi brought his hands together in a clap and the mist and the stream joined together and encased the soldier in a liquid cocoon. Witi lifted him off the ground, turned towards the drones, and prepared to throw.

Wait, Witi!

The voice from the loudspeaker was now a female's. Witi stopped. He looked at Koro and his mum, then back at the drones. Where was Alana? And what was his next move?

A male voice rang out again over the noise:

Stop playing with my soldiers and we'll talk down on the beach. This girl of yours is safe as long as you don't try any more impressive tricks. Understand?

Witi nodded and lowered his hands. The water and the soldier dropped to earth. The soldier tried to catch his breath and the water found its natural flow and disappeared off the ledge like nothing had happened. Witi crouched and placed his hands on his head. He nodded to his mum and Koro to do the same. The drones sank out of sight while one of the soldiers fixed their hands behind their backs with plastic straps.

DON'T LOOK LIKE MUCH OF A THREAT

The beach, where he and Alana and Jordy had stood to survey the surf, now looked like the stage for a full-scale military operation. Four containers – three small and one massive – formed a hub. They were secured to the ground with giant stakes. Electrical cables and wires poured out of the main one and into a series of generators that roared loader than the ocean. The cables flapped and swung in the wind and blown sand. It was like walking onto the set of a modern space movie set in a desert storm. Witi half-expected to see Peter Jackson sitting on his director's chair, eh, a bare foot resting on his other knee, and toking on a hobbit pipe.

But nah, wishful thinking.

There were more military-looking personnel busy doing stuff. They were putting up high-tech equipment that required even more cables. Even more effort to pin them down in the wind.

And there were two giant satellite dishes, each the size of the shed at home. But these weren't looking up at the sky – they were gazing out to sea like they were waiting for something. It didn't look good; they must be big for a reason. They even eclipsed the black helicopter landing next to them. They shook in the wind, but stood strong. Like they were made for these exact weather conditions.

Soldiers walked in pairs, rifles poised over their shoulders. Guess they were expecting danger sometime. From somewhere. Maybe someone.

Pfft, he heard Koro say. That's some high calibre firepower you got there. You boys makin' up for a lack of somethin'?

Bet his mum secretly agreed. Her chin was pushed up and the whites of her eyes were flashing.

She was staunch as. Like she was channelling their ancestors.

But Witi bet their ancestors would just be rolling their eyes at all of this.

Watching the three of them zip-tied up and looking like they were the trespassers.

There was yelling from down towards the high-tide mark where more soldiers were fighting the latest surge of white-water by stacking bags filled with sand in a makeshift wall. Witi listened to the water laugh as it hit the four-foot fortification in an explosion of foam. When it retreated it left sodden, exposed holes in their efforts.

They were led into the heart of the camp. The closer they got the more Witi found his gaze down at his feet. Too many eyes staring, eh. And just at him. Like he was some sort of freak. Outside a steel container they stopped and Koro and his mum were ushered in through a darkened door. Witi went to follow, but the door was closed and he was nudged away. He didn't even get a chance to see inside.

Not you, the soldier said. He pushed Witi down the alleyway between the containers.

From inside the steel walls he heard his mum yell.

Leave him alone! she said. Witi!

There was shuffling of feet and grunts and strains and a thud that sickened him.

Mum! he called back over his shoulder.

But there was no response.

Quiet. The soldier nudged him with the butt of his rifle.

Koro! Witi yelled.

Just silence, except for the sound of Witi being kicked in the back of the legs. He fell forward and his face hit the sand.

I said *quiet.*

Witi spat grains out.

Help him up, he heard a voice say. It was deep and rich and full of authority. It perfectly matched the pointy, shiny black shoes centimetres from his nose.

He was lifted up by the armpits. As he did he saw:

a black pair of suit pants,

a golden belt buckle joining black leather.

The whitest, crispest shirt in the history of ironed shirts, complete with an open top button and sleeves rolled neatly to the elbow.

The man was looking at Witi with interest, with the same blue eyes as Jordy. He ran a hand over his black hair.

He walked around Witi, like he was sizing him up.

Don't look much like any Aquarian I've seen before, he said. So young. Jordy was right for once. He stopped in front of Witi again. You don't look like much of a threat.

He leant forward. He was searching Witi's eyes for something. Witi thought about headbutting him, bang, right in that pointy shnoz of his. But his hands were held in plastic and there were more guys with guns here than some island nation armies had. So he stood there channelling his mum.

Eventually Jordy's dad retreated. But he stopped and suddenly stepped forward again.

What do we have here? He pulled the necklace out from Witi's wetsuit.

He dangled it close to his face and the glow clashed with the blue of his eyes and darkened them. He smiled like a second-hand car salesman.

I thought this was lost with your father, he said, and yanked it free.

Give it back, Witi said.

Oh, I don't think so. This has become a very good day. Put him in a separate container to the others.

No, Witi said, it doesn't belong to you. He struggled with his hands, and threw his shoulders into the first soldier who approached him. But Witi merely bounced off him, so he tried to ram the soldier again. His hands were in a frenzy and felt like they were bleeding. An arm wrapped around his neck and squeezed, cutting off his breath. Blackness was coming, he could feel it.

But he spotted a large drum sitting on a crate. He twisted his hands to one side and with all his might willed whatever liquid was in there to obey his fingers. The drum rattled and shook, like it was coming alive. Then, as his vision faded to grey, the whole container lunged from its setting, flew through the air, and took out the soldier holding him and two of his mates, in one blow.

Witi staggered to his feet. Jordy's dad was just standing there slowly clapping.

You're quite the find, he said. Impressive. And so young.

Get off our land, Witi said between gasps.

Jordy's dad held his hands outstretched and he turned each way. But don't you like what we've done to the place? Check it out. Where's the wind gone? See those dishes? Biggest cyclone your country's seen and we're taming it. Your land would be in ruins within a day if we weren't here. He winked. So you're welcome.

Let us go, Witi said.

You and your Koro.

Wait, what?

The Rastafarian hermit.

You know him?

Your father too. We all have history together. I don't understand how you ended up with the most important artefact, but I'm very glad you did.

What'd you do to him? Witi screamed.

The soldiers were back on their feet and Witi felt their presence closing in. Jordy's dad casually put a hand up to stop them.

Actually what did he do to himself is the correct question. See, you Aquarians are like portals to another dimension. Your father didn't share our vision of future-proofing civilisation with the energy source we were collecting, so he decided to close the door before we could complete the task. Guess he got stuck on the other side. Or maybe he drowned. Take your pick. Anyway, it's been a long eight years since. Heard you were lost to the city. But I had to be sure so Jordy came in handy for once. I'm actually thankful our patience has paid off. My brief was to take care of you if you came close, but with all your young talent and potential to explore, I think holding onto you would be more lucrative. There are many people far from here who would like to see your capacities. And we have the necklace which will look very good for my superiors and my annual bonus. *And*, Mother Nature is here at her most feisty! It's all worked out brilliantly.

Witi ran at him. He'd tear his face off with his teeth if he had to. But he never got a chance.

He felt a blow to the back of his head.

And instant blackness.

DINGO'S FAT HEAD

Witi's sitting on his surfboard in a deep trough between what he now knows to be waves. No more comparisons to the Himalayas or Everest. These are real.

Giants, as silent as ghosts and lethal as the most violent of tornadoes. Hard to imagine such a force of nature. But these are real.

Real as.

And when in their journey they're suddenly greeted by the doorstep of prehistoric reef clinging staunchly to the Earth's crust below, it trips the first wave up.

It topples forward, folding upon itself, creating a cavity that could swallow a ship like a toy in a kid's bath.

While a thick westerly blows the scalp off the wave and throws it back to the horizon.

Back to where it was born, the love child of the sun and a demented, wild wind, a force not seen before, the influence of man upsetting nature's balance.

Nature poked with a stick to see what it would do.

And in these cavities, Witi sees colour. Yes, colour.

Hundreds of silhouettes of people in every shade of every colour.

And there's Dad in front of them all, nodding like he knows what Witi's meant to do.

Until the wave finishes peeling and he and the others disappear, only to reappear within the next wave.

A replica of the last.

Colours and people, in the middle of real giant waves. Calling his name like

Witiii

Yeah.

Wiiiti

Their outlines pulled with the fast-moving water as it goes up and over and explodes in a mass of white and is recycled.

He hasn't a clue what he's meant to do.

All he knows is that his head feels like it needs panel beating and the smell of petrol is thick in the salt air.

When Witi opened his eyes he felt a cool breeze. It was so tranquil he thought he must be camping somewhere. He blinked as he tried to recollect: if Alana was outside; what food they'd brought; what the surf was like; that sorta stuff. Looking around, he saw red plastic containers of petrol stacked high and wide. Sound rushed in and the tranquillity was replaced with the roar of machinery and mayhem outside. He would've covered his ears, but his hands were tied to his feet.

Witiii, he heard, a thin, whispering voice. *Over here.*

Even in the dark of the corner he could identify the outline of Dingo's fat head.

Jesus, you're farkin' deaf, he said. Been calling ya forever.

You gonna get your daddy to hit me again? Witi asked. Piss off.

He's a mad fucker, Jordy said. Even more than usual.

What you want?

To help.

I said piss off.

I ain't a part of this circus. Dad's gone nuts this time. The prick's outta control. Fark 'im.

Jordy was no longer in his wetsuit, but khaki overalls, the same colour as everything else around here. There was a giant embroidered IEP badge on his chest. He was still in bare feet, though, a subtle hint he hadn't been entirely welcomed back.

I gotta find Mum and Koro. Alana too. What do you care?

I know where they are.

Jordy slunk into the shadows behind the petrol containers. Two soldiers entered, grabbed a container each and started crabbing their way out under the weight. One was saying they needed more generators or something, Witi couldn't tell. Didn't matter because when the other soldier saw Witi, the soldier made a quiet shoosh. He faced Witi through his dark glasses the whole time he exited. Witi would've pulled the finger to him if he could've, didn't care if it resulted in another black-out. But maybe Jordy was telling the truth, so he resorted to a mean stink-eye instead.

Once they left, Jordy was suddenly in his face.

Here, gimme ya mitts, he said.

He pushed Witi onto his stomach and sawed open the ties.

Witi rubbed his wrists where the plastic had cut the skin.

C'mon, Jordy said, pulling at Witi's arm. This way. Before they get back.

I'm not trustin' ya.

And there's no time to convince you. But I know where everyone is. I know they'll kill you if you stay here. And I know if you don't stop this madness, we're *all* farked.

At the opening of the enclosure he peered outside.

Hurry up, mate, he whispered.

They snuck back down the lane between the steel boxes. Witi couldn't remember which one his mum and Koro were in, but when Jordy put a hand to Witi's chest and told him to wait a sec, he knew they must be close. Jordy darted across to the container opposite and crawled alongside it like some sorta rodent. Amongst the whine of technology, he disappeared around the corner. He reappeared with a smile and a thumbs-up like it was the most fun he'd had this whole nutted-out trip. He motioned Witi to follow and vanished around the corner again.

Witi waited in the shadows for the laneway to clear. Two men in uniform were crossing paths with a third. They stopped near Witi and spoke loudly over the wind:

First soldier: The wind is currently sitting at eighty-two clicks and dropping at a rate of ten every ten. The swell's peaking at fifteen hundred-oh-eight, sir.

Third soldier: Is everything in place?

First soldier: We're confident it is.

Third soldier: Confident? What's that supposed to mean?

Second soldier: Well, Terry down at Sector Six has been training two new recruits. This cyclone is playing havoc with them. Apparently millennials don't like the sand getting in their gear, sir.

First Soldier: One of them's Johnny's nephew.

Second Soldier: Johnny in the workshop or Johnny down at Perimeter Defence?

First Soldier: The second.

Second Soldier: Heard he almost got thrown into one of the drones earlier on by that magic kid.

Third Soldier: Thirteen hundred-oh-eight is exactly forty minutes from now. Within ten minutes I want to see a checklist ticked and signed off from every manager down on the site, that everything is in place. Are you *confident* you're hearing me?

They nodded, turned and broke into a jog. The third soldier stood there and held a phone to his head.

Everything is in place, sir ... Do you want me to get rid of the kid and his family now? ... Bring the kid to you first, dispose of the others? Not a problem.

When he cleared the way, Witi scampered on hands and feet across the lane and into the other shipping container.

IT'S EVOLUTION

Koro had Jordy on the ground. Sitting on him and twisting his arm high up his back while whispering his ear. When Witi's mum saw her son she took him in a hug.

What's he doing? Witi asked.

It's okay, lad, he's gonna spill the beans, ain't ya?

Jordy was grimacing, obviously stifling a yell, but under the circumstances he was holding it in for everyone's sake.

Get him off me, Witi, he managed to say.

He was gonna make life worse for us, Koro said.

I was gonna untie you.

Well, I untied myself, so surprise.

Witi told Koro what he'd heard. This was the first place they'd be looking. He pointed at Jordy: And he knows where Alana is.

Koro didn't look that happy to have his interrogation interrupted, but he rolled off Jordy, stood up and offered a giant hand to pull him to his feet.

I'm only doin' it for the lad, he said. And that lass of his.

Check the two in this box!

You gotta split, Jordy told Witi. I'll stay here with them.

Where is she? Witi asked.

My dad's container, the last one, closest inland.

Why's she ...?

It's not important. Get outta here.

Koro nodded. He had a deep red and purple swelling on his fore-head. You could just about see the rifle butt's imprint.

We'll be okay, Koro said.

Mum nodded.

Witi fled for the doorway.

Shit, almost forgot, said Jordy. 2001, remember it. Dad's combo.

Since Witi heard the soldiers entering from the left, he slunk out the right side. Just in time as he heard Jordy's best surprised voice welcoming them.

The last shipping container Jordy had referred to was the busiest of the lot.

Witi had crawled and rolled, skidded and crept his way to this point, but no way could he get past all the people loitering around the opening. The front doors were his only option. But how ...

How was he gonna make them go?

Past the giant machines on stilts with their barrels and coils point-ing out to sea,

he saw the tide leaking through the sacks stacked man-height.

And he thought,

what if ...?

Could I?

The ocean?

Am I capable?

That sorta stuff.

He closed his eyes, and imagined he was drawing the ocean towards him. His hands made the motion of pulling on a massive rope, like the ones holding ships to berth.

The rumble and yells of panic came quickly as the barricade of bags toppled and dark figures ran. A fortress wall of white water stampeded over the foreshore, the sound of a symphony growing louder and louder, drowning out the screams of everyone in its path. A couple of soldiers managed to flee but the rest were swallowed and carried past Witi, out of sight. The water tumbled up to the main container but stopped when Witi lowered his hands and let his thoughts go. The ocean drained back, leaving its bedraggled pathway. Witi made his move.

It was dark inside, darker than the other steel boxes he'd been in. This one was twice as large too, and felt more solid as the wind struggled to shake it. But there were pockets of yellow from the halogen lamps, one on the solid wooden desk across the far side, another lighting up a giant whiteboard, and a couple sitting on a large table in the middle of the room. He couldn't tell if anyone else was here, but it looked like there was nowhere to hide.

Babe, he whispered as he did his best ninja walk, *you here?*

Witi was drawn to the whiteboard, with its curious scribbles and drawings. He read the cryptic notes, guessing his way through the diagrams:

circles within circles, someone drawing Trudy, he guessed.

A topography map, the reef formation, a massive red X where he reckoned they'd been surfing.

A couple of circles on stick legs – quick sketches of the two big satellite-type contraptions – drawn on the coast. They had arrows pointing out to sea and a shitty attempt at a wave. From that picture even bigger arrows like squiggly vibration symbols pointed towards a few squares with lines and coils back on land. And beside these was an equals symbol and two fat dollar signs.

Heaps of letters without vowels and random numbers everywhere. Like someone was talking android. Real foreign stuff, except for 8003008. He'd seen that little combo before.

Wished it came with some footnote somewhere, a website address, a word or two even.

He heard anxious voices approaching. He spun in circles looking for the best place to exit, but containers weren't designed with escape hatches. As a last resort he buckled, slid under the desk, and tucked himself into the corner, pulling his knees in tight to stop his goofy feet showing.

Let me talk to him, he'll listen to me.

Alana's voice sounded like at home. Man, if only he was with her.

I want him back, he heard that new deep voice say. How well do you know him, Alana?

Jordy's dad was looking for something. His fingers flicked over documents and moved piles. I mean, really know him?

Forever.

Forever? Forever is a long time, Alana, but it's merely a concept. It's no longer than the cycle of life, he said, and there was a sudden loud slap on the desk top above Witi's head. Shorter than this fly's stint in this world. An attempt by the English language to control time. I've only met you for a matter of hours yet I know you're searching for a solution, another chance, like so many others. Parents forced into uprooting a life to find a new one in a more prosperous place. That place will die too. Forever has nothing to do with it. No, what I asked, Alana, is how well do you know Witi?

There was silence, until Witi wondered if she'd left the room. Then:

He's quiet. Has a sensitive disposition. He's never felt complete since his dad left. I never met him, but I know he's in Witi, you can just sorta tell. His thoughts are fragmented and beautiful. He writes songs for me and I feel safe. That enough?

Did you know he was a guardian?

I don't think he knew himself.

He would've known all right.

He never said anything.

You would've seen it.

Seen what?

This.

What were they looking at? Witi wished he could've poked his head

up. All he could hear was faint breathing from Alana, getting quicker.

His father was one, he finally heard her say.

Yes, that's correct. An extraordinary one. Quite the rock-star life he led. He fell in love. Our experience with his type suggests he was an outlier.

Does that make Witi one?

Turns out it does, he said, and a very special one at that. It's the first time we've known of a guardian having a child.

He stopped the flow of a flooded river. I was trapped. I would've died.

These Aquarians, gate keepers, whatever you want to call them, have been on this Earth since mankind first left a footprint on the low-tide mark. Thanks to my late wife's research, we know their basic role is to ensure that doorways to the next life are not exposed to the rest of the human race. But we, you and I, have evolved with technology to a point where we need a new energy source in order to survive. The energy created from something like an event such as this, if we could capture that, Alana, you, your parents, and billions of others could survive in comfort. So it's simple: those who have the most powerful source stand to make the most from life. Think about that, Alana – a better life, forever.

There was silence again and Witi willed Alana not to get sucked in.

You want the best for your parents? A future family? More opportunities for your own children than you ever imagined you could offer?

More silence. Finally:

Yeah, course I do.

Yes, he said, chuckling, yes. Of course you do. I want you to have that too.

But what about Witi?

Well, that's up to you, Alana. You've seen what he's capable of. He's far more dangerous than you know, and who knows where he is right now. He could be angry, confused – or, even worse, scared. His power is fascinating, but unstable. That's why I had to relieve him of the carving around his neck.

Where is it?

Locked away. Safe. Where it won't hurt anyone.

He'd never hurt me, or anyone. He's a little odd at times, but he's a teenager like the rest of us. Doesn't make him a freak.

Witi heard a thump like hands on a surface.

He stands for an antiquated idealism! The tide of power has changed. Humans have grown and matured to this moment in time. Don't you see, Alana? This is not good versus bad, it's evolution. We have the chance to control our destiny, become self-sufficient. You think some mystical power is going to save us from the effects of climate change? From recession after recession? From drought and flood or disease and starvation? We have a chance to redeem ourselves in the light of our forefathers' fossil-fuelled banquet of the last one hundred years. This swell isn't like any swell – no, man's greed has stirred this puppy up. Turned the dial past what nature intended. The intensity it brings is opening the door and now is the time to collect.

You talking about climate change? Alana asked.

Yes.

And it's a *good thing*?

Yes.

You're not just on the crazy train, you're driving it.

In times of great despair are great opportunities. Climate change isn't going to destroy us. It's going to redeem humankind. We now have that technology, to capture the energy for everyone. You're just a kid, but even you must appreciate what we're about to do.

This time Witi was convinced she'd bolted, buggered off outta there. He sure as heck would've. But Jordy's dad continued in a different tone, like he was just another dad.

You love him, don't you?

More silence, and again he wished he coulda stuck his head up.

Hmm, Jordy's dad said. Figured as much.

There were footsteps and suddenly the man was behind the desk. He sat on the chair and Witi saw the large pistol in his hand and resting on his lap. Jordy's dad crossed his legs, his black shoe rocking back and forth towards Witi. It was so close he could see the outline of his head in its shine.

I'm not going to hurt him, if that's what you're worried about, Jordy's dad said. I merely want to make sure he stays out of harm's way while we finish the job we were sent here to do. He tapped the top of the gun with his index finger as he spoke. You trust me, don't you?

No, she said, and Jordy's dad's fingers tightened their grip on the pistol.

But ...

Yes? His fingers retracting.

But will you guarantee my parents will be looked after, and we can stay where we are? They'll have jobs and that?

They'll have all the security they need. They can build another storey on the house if they want.

And Witi's mum and granddad, they'll be free to go afterwards?

I'll have them dropped off on their front lawn in my own jetcopter, not a problem.

And Witi ...

As I said, he won't be harmed. You'll be with him within minutes of the completed task.

Then ...then, yeah. I'll help you find him.

MY CUZ AND THE PRETTY WAHINE

Jordy's dad stood and put the pistol inside his jacket. He walked back around the desk and Witi could tell by the sound of his steps that he was pleased with himself. Pleased with progress.

Witi waited beneath the desk until he was sure they'd left. Too bad he hadn't been able to give Alana a sign, to let her know that whatever state she thought he was in, he was still just normal old Witi and she had nothing to worry about ... except that she'd just made a pact with all things that make mankind its own worst enemy. But he couldn't, not with Jordy's old man running around, his finger on the trigger. Witi was on his own.

Whatever he was meant to do, Witi needed his carving back. He started rummaging through the equipment and gear, boxes and files. The safe, he figured. Where else would it be? He started off working delicately, but he thought of his dad trapped in that cave, and how long he'd waited to leave. He thought of the way they'd been bonded by the carvings, by DNA and by music and so much more he never knew because it was denied to him. Well, he was soon throwing boxes, pushing over file cabinets and kicking at gear and equipment. All the noise was hidden by the racket of an aggressive ocean. He paused only once, to pick up a framed picture from the desk, of a woman in outdoor clothing, like she was hiking somewhere tropical judging from the monkeys watching her. Except that the clipboard showed she might have been working. She looked elegant, in a rugged sorta way. It was a brief moment of compassion from Witi for Jordy, and he placed the photo gently back. The rest of the place looked like Cyclone Trudy had entered and had her way.

Hey there, he said, wiping sweat from his eyes, or it coulda been tears. Taken your time.

The fantail sliced through the air as it circled the inside of the container. It landed on a surfboard cover and Witi couldn't believe he hadn't seen that earlier. It was more or less camouflaged in the gloom of the room. He navigated the mess and ripped the fabric from the board. His dad's green surfboard. Jordy must've brought it back. In this moment it comforted him, a little piece of heirloom in a tough situation. He picked it up by its rails and rested it for a moment on his forehead. Next thing, he noticed that it had been covering a large safe box with a digital key pad. He knelt down and pushed

2

0

0

1

There was a tiny whirr and a click and the door opened.

Inside the safe, lying modestly on the steel surface, was the necklace, glowing blue within the shadows of its silver confines. He plucked it out and hung it back around his neck, instantly feeling the surge flow through his blood again. And he felt a familiarity – a synergy – with the air that he breathed. The fog cleared in his mind. He felt more stable in his posture.

He twirled on the spot and landed a sweet kick on the door to shut it. Suddenly a piercing alarm rang out from a speaker, letting everyone know someone was where they shouldn't be. Witi grabbed the old man's board, tucked it under his arm and ran for the door.

But these guys moved with military precision. Must've had twenty or more barrels already pointing at him every which way he looked as he exited the container.

Go figure, eh. They didn't give those guns out to the type of people you found on a production line.

Their steely faces glared through giant scopes; musta seen his innards with that much power. Probably watching his heart beat faster.

He turned on the spot, seeking any exit. But all he saw was

black masks, black balaclavas, black uniforms and shiny black boots.

Some soldiers extra shiny from the water still dripping off them.

One guy's tongue lightly running the length of a lip.

Yeah, they still looked pissed with him.

Like they could happily slice a bullet through any one of his vital organs.

They were just waiting on him to make a stupid move.

Waiting for an excuse.

To put him out of the picture.

'Cos they had a job to do and all that.

This coulda been one of those Mexican stand-off scenarios. But even if he called for the ocean to bail him out again, by the time it arrived he'd have more holes than the surfboard he was clutching. Slow and controlled, he raised the old man's board above his head and gave his most earnest smile ever.

Don't shoot the freak, he yelled over the wind.

When Alana saw Witi, she broke through the wall of bodies. She put herself in front of Witi, held her hands up and yelled at the soldiers to lower their guns. She turned to face Witi.

I thought you'd long gone, she said. I didn't know where to start looking for you.

She moved in closer. This was about to turn into a good day.

Next time I'm calling the shots, she said, and whacked his chest.

Very sentimental, but the reunion's over. Jordy's dad had turned up. He stared at his watch and whispered orders to someone.

Alana grabbed Witi's bicep. It's okay, she told him, we're free to leave now. He gave me his word.

Bind those two together and put them in a container, furthest from any blasted water, Jordy's dad said. Lock the door, bolt it shut this time and I want you, you, and you guarding the entrance. The boy needs to be prepared for a big trip and he's not to miss it.

But you ... Alana protested.

Jordy's dad smiled and Witi saw the resemblance to Jordy. Having the time of his life, eh. He turned and left with a posse behind him. Alana was pulled from Witi by two of the soldiers. She struggled as they led her away. Four others surrounded Witi with their rifles and walked him in the same direction.

Witi's brain was working overtime. He'd never been the best at problem solving—hadn't had to use that part of his brain much before the last few days. The fact that none of them were hurt ... well, that was promising. Maybe he was doin' okay with being thrown in the deep end, but yeah. This little turn of events wasn't gonna look great on his scorecard. He'd seen those shipping containers and it wouldn't be so easy to get out of one the second time.

When they turned the corner the front group stopped. There was a Māori man, moko over his face and hair as wild as his eyes which were staring at the soldiers. He stood legs apart, wearing a pair of boardies and black t-shirt. A short pig-hunting rifle rested on his crossed arms.

Who are you? The first soldier aiming his gun at him.

The stranger pointed a large finger and the group of soldiers parted until it was aiming straight at Witi.

His cuz, the guy said. Give him and his missus to me now.

That's not going to happen, the soldier said. He walked on ... and was stopped by the barrel of the man's rifle.

Don't think you're hearing me, trespasser. I want my cuz and the pretty wahine.

The soldier swung out with the butt of his gun, but the man deftly sidestepped it and jabbed the butt of his own into the soldier's face, smashing the goggles and dropping him to the ground. He swivelled his rifle around and pointed it at the remaining soldiers now doing the same back to him.

And just when Witi thought they were about to witness the death of possibly the bravest family member he'd never known, clicks sounded all around. They found themselves surrounded by Māori men with moko and guns, taiaha, boardies and black Ts. Musta been twice as many as there were soldiers.

Had there ever been such a stealth ambush before?

A war party his ancestors would be proud of.

Koro stepped forward, and Witi saw his mum standing behind.

You boys better give us those rifles before you hurt someone, Koro told the soldiers.

There was an uncertain pause from the troops. But when the first one surrendered his arms, the others followed.

C'mon, you two, Koro said to Witi and Alana, you're with us.

Jordy was there too. Standing back a bit, still wary of everyone, eh. I'll hang here, try to create a diversion, he said. Give ya some time to scarper.

Thanks, Witi said, but he didn't mean it a hundred.

As they were swallowed by the whānau, his mum stepped up and walked around each soldier with that fierce look on her face. She stopped in front of one.

Looked at him real close like. Yeah, you're him, she said.

Then she decked him so hard the guy behind had to support him back to his feet.

A real warrior never hits a wahine, she said.

THE ONE DIMENSION

They fled over the sand for the safety of the bush. There was a huge boom behind them and Witi looked back. Jordy must've had some fun with that container full of petrol because now it was all flames and thick smoke.

They entered the bush and started climbing. When they'd got far enough up and away, Koro stopped them.

He hadn't finished with Witi.

You still have a job to do, lad, he told him. You know this.

And Witi glanced around at the faces of his cousins and uncles, all with the same silent look, like they knew what had to be done. He looked at his mum and there was a quiver in her eyes, but she was still staunch and for just a sec he thought he saw a deeper feeling, like she was holding back an element of denial. She never knew that he could see his dad's faint aura, but now his dad's hand was on her shoulder and with her next exhale she gave a shrug, as if accepting something inevitable. Was this, whatever was about to happen, what his mum had hoped to protect him from all along?

But that conversation could wait. A commotion was coming from the camp below, even through the wind in the trees around them. Orders were being yelled, machines started, the high pitch of drone blades turning. One of the cousins ran back to the huddle:

There's a group headin' up, he said.

You have to shut the door, Koro continued, pointing one of his giant fingers at Witi.

How? he asked. I don't get it.

The last set wave at the peak of the swell will produce Te Kore inside its cavity. It's a door to the other side, where our wairua goes when we die. Imagine that, lad, the energy source of all life on Earth, captured in the one dimension. Your mate Jordy's old man sure can. Koro scratched a wave in the dirt, and scratched a cross in the barrel. This is where you need to be at the time when that wave rises. You are a key. You must close the entrance before those guys get in.

The first gun shot rang out and they all flinched. All except Koro.

Look at the picture, lad. Do you understand me?

Witi nodded.

Tell me you do.

Yes, he said, but I don't. I mean, how can I know which set is the last? And even then ...then what? It's a wave, it doesn't have a door handle.

Your father knew, Mum said. You will too.

Koro pointed at Witi's chest. That will tell you, he said.

Their own group started returning shots, but into the air to give the impression they were raining bullets back. The smiles said they were dealing the ultimate stitch-up.

Koro handed Witi the green surfboard. You have to go, he said. Head down there through the bracken, and take the dry creek bed to the beach. Run across the sand and paddle straight out through

the channel in the reef. It's around the point. They shouldn't see you.
We'll keep their attention here as we head on up.

Love you, son, Mum said.

Wait, Alana yelled. I'm coming too.

No, lass, there's nothing you can do.

Man, did she look frustrated.

Sure I can ...

Stay with us, Witi's mum told her.

Witi went and put his hand to Alana's face. He kissed her lips. He
hugged her. Love you, babe, always have, he said. He stood back and
she was smiling at him.

Don't call me that, she said, and hurry back.

As Witi crawled through the ferns where Koro had shown him, and
his bare feet stepped over the cold, rounded river stones, he wondered whether Koro had been pointing at the necklace or his heart
and which one was supposed to provide him with the answer.

Had he known the eeriness that would greet him when he stepped
onto the beach Witi would've risked bumming the whānau out by
saying nah to Koro and heading home. It seemed Jordy's dad and
his crew had done the impossible. They had turned the wind into a
controlled breeze, juxtaposed against the circling grey sky with its
strands of lightning and the roaring ocean thunder. But he was here
and there was no turning back.

He strode and leapt into the water until he couldn't stand against the surge and started paddling with furious strokes. The ocean was a thousand shades of dark. Something had died, it seemed. Even the giant scalps at the tops of each wave, previously a flashy white, were now morbid grey. Like the warmth of skin lost on someone's death-bed.

His hands propelled him forward but the water felt inert. Maybe others wouldn't've noticed it, let alone felt it, but he did. The way those same people would notice if their air was contaminated. It wasn't oily, or thicker or thinner. It didn't smell any different and the sting of salt still lingered in the cracks of his lips. But it definitely felt dead. Its wairua was leaving, or had already left.

What really gave it away, though, was the silence. No whispers, no name, no music. Just the cry of cold black water tumbling towards land.

Witi felt the first of the pulses halfway out to the breaking waves. Like being hit from some sort of power source. It sent surges through his whole body, and after each surge Witi's limbs cramped, he lost strength and he struggled even to move. He felt for the necklace and pressed it harder against his skin. He knew it was trying to restore his energy.

Behind him on the land, the campsite was still visible. The machines perched on the sand and staring out to sea must be sucking the life force from whatever fell within their gaze. Including Witi.

He pushed the front of the board into the approaching wall of wave and pierced his way through its flesh. He exhaled through his nostrils and held his eyes open, trying to make sense of the black water as the mass swept around him. He broke through to the other side and filled his lungs with air.

He sat up on the surfboard in the channel and watched the next set of waves roll in. The first kept rising higher and in his feet he felt the suck and twist of water as the wave commanded more and more water to join its mass of energy. Giant, thick slabs of water, menacing, intimidating and mortally draining. Completely out of his league at any other time. He wanted to feel scared; it would have been normal. But he only felt numb, like a storm of nothingness had swept through his body and washed the important parts away. Like he'd lost all emotion.

Felt as inert as the surfboard he was sitting on.

He was just staring at the task ahead, one wave crashing down like thunder

while the next grew huge and stared back at the kid on the old dunger of a board.

Could he even paddle this board into something so big?

Koro said his dad had. Made it sing, he reckoned.

Witi looked at his scoops. Man, he'd paddled into a wave or two more than most with these.

He glanced back at the beach. Couldn't believe what he seeing. Jordy paddling out towards him. He wasn't grinning or anything, just glaring at Witi with a grimace like something was holding him back. He paddled in beside Witi and sat up.

...he said.

...body convulsed like something was sweeping through it.
...ed like he was trying to hide the pain.

Whaddya doin' here? Witi asked.

You gonna finish this thing or what?

Witi looked back at the waves. I'm kinda scared, he said. He turned to him. Scared of failing.

Two black drones came down off the hills above the cove and rather than hover over the camp, sped out towards them. They gave off flashes of light and the surfers felt the sensation of heavy rain.

Whatever you gotta do, do it quickly. Jordy got onto his stomach and paddled towards the waves. They can't have you interfering. They're gonna kill you.

Where you going? Witi called.

I'll double ya chances. Hopefully they won't be able to tell who's who in the chaos.

The drones flew closer but their controller hadn't taken into account the size of the waves. Witi saw them go behind a wave and only one lifted over it in time. The other disappeared into the trough, like the sea had swallowed it. Flashes of yellow came from the remaining craft as it continued towards them.

Witi sat on his board and closed his eyes.

With his hands he imagined he was grabbing fistfuls of ocean.

He heard the whirr of the rotors and the scream of the engine, and when he sensed the timing was right and that the might of the ocean was on his side, he raised his hands and opened his eyes to catch the drone in his watery mitts.

But this time he was just a kid sitting on a dunger.

With a coupla scoops raised above his head.

Like some sorta smart-ass gesture – take ya best shot, dickheads.

Whatever was draining the energy had left his ability high and dry too.

The first bullets pinged through the water like a dotted line and into the front of the fibreglass.

And forced him to abandon his board and swim deep into the mute blackness.

Hoping that none of the bullets tunnelling beside him would find their target.

When his ears couldn't take any more equalising, he stopped and hovered in the darkness until the shots finished, and he figured he was out of range.

But then the last bullet hit his upper chest and pushed him deeper into the blackness and he let out a yell of despair, pissed off that it had to end like this. Pissed off that his last taste of oxygen was heading back to the surface in a trail of bubbles.

I'M FINISHED ALL RIGHT

Turquoise.

That's what greeted Witi when he opened his eyes.

Sweet, turquoise. Illuminated like stained glass in a church. Or a secluded wave on a forgotten reef pass. And he felt her touch on the back of his neck and the tightness of steel strings under his thumb.

Then he must've passed out again.

What's happened to me?

He was asking the silhouette staring down at him. The light blue-green outline of someone. An adult. Male.

Am I dead?

The figure continued staring, barely moving in the shiny whiteness. Just kinda shimmered there until he placed a hand on Witi's chest and there was a tingling warmth on his skin. A finger entered the hole where the bullet had broken through his flesh and left a path through him; he knew this because he felt the finger creep through his muscle, barely missing his heart and spine, and stop on his back. No pain at all, just warmth. The figure's hand fell back to his side and when Witi put his own hand up to the wound all that greeted him was smooth skin. Like that last bullet had missed him altogether.

No pal, you're not dead.

I can't see you. Why?

You're not finished yet.

I got shot. I drowned. It's a double blow. I'm **finished, all right.**

You die, the world dies. We die.

And Witi saw the white background become a **forest of silhou**ettes, so that soon the rare haze of white was the only other **colour** he saw. His dad had disappeared, or merged, into the one colour **with** everyone or everything else around him. Witi could feel the **warmth** on his hand, the only evidence his father was still beside him.

Who are they? Witi asked.

Descendants, your ancestors, souls you'll never know. Here to see you succeed. You mustn't fail. Without them, there's nothing.

Where have you been?

I couldn't beat them, the ones who want to exploit the power. I had no choice but to shut the door before I could get back out. I'm still here.

But what should I do?

The living are taking the energy from the ocean. If the wairua of the ocean dies they'll be able to pass into the next world. Their future world. Without the energy in the wave, they'll be free to do this. You have to re-ignite the life-force and close the door between worlds.

How though? I don't get it.

There are vibrations in the wave. Sound vibrations. These control the door.

The white started turning grey. His dad was fading.

... still ... released ...

... what? Dad!

The grey was swapped for darkness as Witi blacked out.

When Witi opened his eyes the day seemed so much brighter than he remembered. This must be how it was when you'd died and been involved in a miracle – you saw things in a new way all of a sudden. Sure, dirty clouds were still sitting above him, but as he floated on his back out in the calm channel of ocean away from the impact zone and breathed his first taste of air, man, he was smiling for the first time in ages. Especially when he felt a nudge at the back of his skull. He climbed onto the green board and fingered the new bullet holes – proof that he hadn't just had a trippy turn of some sort. He leant over and sank his face into the water and stared into the blackness. He felt them – those souls and his dad – staring back. Willing him on towards a destiny.

Witi looked all around but there was no sign of Jordy. Nothing. He half expected to see the tiny black outline of his body cutting down the face of the latest set wave, but it broke unscathed like so many before it. The drone held no clues either; it seemed to have gotten bored – or finished – with the task at hand and was making its way back to shore. Leaving Witi floating out here all alone. On the surface, anyway.

He sat up on the board. It rose and fell with the swell, but he was just out of the impact zone. And for the first time ever, the thought of donning a pair of sprigged boots and trying his chances against the rugby-heads at school actually seemed like a better scenario than what he was currently contemplating.

Man, if they could see him now.

Maybe Jordy was right, maybe they would put Witi in brass at the college gates.

Yeah, probably as a memorial.

He looked around again for a sign of Jordy and this time he caught a glimpse of Jordy's board drifting alone in the distance amongst the ocean chop. Witi stared, looking for an outstretched hand, but he knew that miracles like the one he'd just experienced only happened once. A memorial statue? Better make that two.

He watched the next set heave in, and each of its waves erupting, one after the after. His chest started tingling like he had a mobile phone set on vibrate down there. As the second and third waves passed through, the sensation built in intensity. By the last wave – the biggest he'd seen, way bigger than he ever thought he'd dare to be this close to – it felt like a burning stake being driven through his chest. Witi clutched at the necklace and felt the heat through his wetsuit. It was telling him what he had to know.

A RAIDING TITAN

The ocean went flat after that. A slight pulse heading to the shore was the only evidence of something lurking.

But it was just a break between waves, a long period swell generated by Trudy hanging out over the horizon. Must've been twenty or even thirty seconds long. The big periods made deep troughs between the sets, the sort that took inexperienced boaties too close to underwater reefs. The waves on either side of a period break rose like no other force in the world – some scary shit to see from behind the steering wheel. Not that anyone else would've been out here. Just some teenager starting to paddle as fast as he could to get into the best position, the deepest he could be, into the take-off zone. And there he waited and stared out into the open ocean, watching for that first sign of a black rise in the horizon.

Seemed like forever. And finally, it came.

Like he'd been sitting quietly in the middle of the bus lane on a busy motorway, waiting for the inevitable.

He paddled out to meet it.

Couldn't help it, the fearful thought of being too deep. Jesus. He'd already experienced dying once today.

Didn't need to push his luck.

He could feel the tingling, the carving's way of talking to him. And he knew.

This was it. What he was meant to do. Where he was meant to be.

The wall of water ate away the sky and now he was paddling up, steeply and silently and over.

When he came down, sunlit spray fell around him like an early summer thunderstorm with a giant circular rainbow in it.

But the colours quickly left and a dark presence grew: the next wave looked like a raiding titan approaching through the haze.

And looming beyond it – some eighty feet high – was the terrifying dark mass of the last wave in the set.

OTHER PLANS FOR HIM

The face of the wave caught the late-day sun, making every ripple, every tiny twitch on the beast's watery surface dance like the Milky Way. It caught and held Witi, wide-eyed and mesmerised. The water pulling him in. If he was gonna die again today, there was no more beautifully epic way to go out than to be swallowed by such a hulk of moving matter. The thought horrified and excited him equally. He turned his board down the wave and began paddling. It was surreal, losing all points of reference – no sound, no faces of others to warn him, just the water resisting his paddles as it sucked him up and backwards.

The back of the green surfboard rose as the wave lifted him in its momentum. The wave took him higher, the nose of the board angled steeper and the water under him began to accelerate. He scooped massive handfuls, trying to match the speed. His goofy feet kicked in a frenzy. And still he was going higher. The wave steepened. Higher than the hills back on shore. He just couldn't quite sync himself with the wave.

It was either gonna roll underneath him and leave him in its path.

Or the lip was gonna hook him as it lost its fight with gravity and he'd be devoured deep within the ocean's intestines. There was nothing beautiful about that anymore.

He drove his hands harder and faster and got low on the board and strained so hard he felt his teeth cut into his lip. But still he climbed higher and began to feel the extra, anchoring weight of failure.

The necklace though …

The necklace had other plans for him, he guessed.

Earlier its power had taken a back seat, what with the eighty feet of water he was trying to mount and all that.

But now it was making a noise, a hum. Like a harmonica or some reed instrument.

A vibration.

The first sparks started then. Not the sun, but the lights, the colours. And the whispers.

Stand.

That's what he heard.

Stand.

So he did. Sprang to his feet and tensed for the freefall. But instead of the chaos of wave chatter and gravity, he felt the wave slow and he was gliding down its giant face. He ran his fingers along the inside wall and heard again the chimes of the music. He moved his hands like an artist sculpting the wave's surface, and when he spread them wide the wave resumed its original speed and he had to rely on the traction of fifteen-year-old wax and goofy feet to stay put. When he brought his hands together, the ocean slowed once more. Rainbow sparks leapt from his fingers, surrounding him in colour, and a chorus of joyous song echoed throughout the chamber as the wave boiled over him. He was immersed in reds and blues, pinks and greens. Yellows like forgotten specks of sunshine. The singing boisterous and jubilant. Like a flickering school of fish, coloured figures shimmered under and over him, flowing with the curve of the wave. Hands high in celebration. Yeah, they knew. They saw the radiance of the carving bouncing on his chest.

It was like the ocean had channelled its full might into the one rolling mass. And Witi was controlling it. Him. And the green surfboard with the dings and exposed shards of fibreglass. The singing blended with the roar of the colours as they cascaded over him and smashed into the reef. Everything sounded in sync. He felt no fear. Not for his safety or for not knowing what to do. His dad had made this board sing.

If Koro could see him now!

He railed the board upwards and carved a giant arc back under the dense lip, producing a melody that might've come from an orchestra. When he faced back into the wave he saw the spirits massed in a vast crowd. They raised their hands again and some clapped and things became clearer.

He played that wave. Man, as hard as it was to believe.

Biggest wave, he reckoned, for ever. Musta been.

And he played it like he was on stage with his guitar. Dad's guitar.

He arced and turned, drove up and sped down. Moves like power chords. He buried his hands into the wall and slowed the wave down and got so deep in the barrel he was amongst the spirits.

In the crowd

he felt their hands on his body

and their wairua, still there, still alive.

The wave and the music were unlocking a new energy. And at the same time locking what was always meant to remain secure.

Te Kore, the gateway to beyond. The gateway to the afterlife.

As the carving on his chest blazed.

From high on the green face, he saw soldiers running on the beach as the wave approached. Scrambling for higher ground, scattering up into the bush. They left the cannons pointing, blank and still.

Must've looked like something from an apocalyptic movie coming for them. One of those far-fetched disaster movies where Mother Nature bites back.

When the wave made ground it took everything out: the shipping containers, the remaining helicopters, the cannons and structures. All of it, like it was all made of twigs and cardboard.

Witi surfed through the middle of the destruction. Controlling his speed and descent until the wave lowered him like he was being presented, and the board settled neatly on land. He stepped off and felt sand under his feet. He turned to watch the wave retreating back into the ocean, taking the debris with it. Like it was never there. Wiping the evidence.

TRIED TO SAY GOODBYE

It was strange, standing here by himself. Casting a sole shadow where so much had happened. Only the sound of ocean behind him and the far cry of thunder inland proved he wasn't trapped in some giant screenshot. Even the wind seemed to have dropped. Yeah, he was alone, yet he felt the comforting presence of his ancestors every-where.

Witi!

Alana was running out onto the sandy bay. Her smile met him way before the rest of her did.

That was sick! he thought he heard her say. She wouldn't have been wrong.

She stood in front of Witi, puffing.

Who are you? she asked, searching his eyes. She musta got sick of waiting 'cos she kissed him. It was like the last tidal surge had hauled everything else away, leaving just the two of them alone.

Except for the feeling that his ancestors were watching, eh.

And when he opened an eye to check, there were Koro and his mum and the rest of the whānau standing there. All watching him with the same stupid grin. His mum was the first to come and give him the longest hug. The rest of the group surrounded him with pats and hand-clasps and enough kudos to last him the rest of his life.

The group parted and Koro approached. He held out a massive hand which devoured his own. Koro pulled him close and held him by the shoulder.

A sudden loud crack startled them. It echoed around the bay. Everyone cowered and Witi thought Koro had too, pulling Witi down with his weight. But there was no grip in the hand that fell from Witi's shoulder. Koro's other hand was lifeless in Witi's. His head fell to one side, his dreadlocks still. There was no motion except for the red soaking through his shirt front.

Koro! Witi cried. No!

He grasped Koro by his armpits and tried to lift him, willing him to stand. But no power of Witi's could change this. Koro's weight pulled Witi to his knees. When Koro rolled to his side Witi saw where a bullet had entered his upper back. His mum was suddenly at Witi's side, taking Koro from him. Her cries of grief rose on the air.

Witi stared in confusion at his bloodied hands.

Looking up, he saw Jordy's dad on the bush edge, pistol still pointing directly at Witi. Behind him were soldiers, rifles ready, approaching with caution. Not Jordy's dad, though, who strode purposefully over. His suit was wet and torn, exposing a bloodied thigh. He paced right through their group, his face a mess of scrapes and bruising. His hair was matted and he wore only one shoe.

Witi stood to meet him. Seemed like everyone was waiting for him to do something.

The pistol stopped at Witi's forehead and a faint stream of haze escaped from the muzzle. The soldiers surrounded their group.

Conjure the ocean, Jordy's dad taunted as he pulled back the hammer. I dare you.

Witi closed his eyes. This must be the end.

Jordy's dad had already shot Koro, but he'd probably been aiming for Witi.

Stood to reason he'd shoot him next.

In front of his mum

and Alana,

his whānau and ancestors.

Amazing what the mind could process in just a second.

Waiting for the explosion of gunpowder. The last sound he'd ever hear. His face squeezed tight. Like maybe there was a chance it was only gonna sting a bit.

Dad! he heard to his left. *Stop!*

Witi opened an eye.

Jordy had broken past the soldiers and the family to stand beside Witi. He looked drained, like he'd been stuck in the bravado-beating machine on spin cycle. He collapsed onto one knee, too weak to stand.

For fark's sake, Dad, he said between breaths. Put it down.

Witi sensed Jordy's dad hesitate, compromised by the sight of his son. Surely he'd thought the same as everyone else, that Jordy had drowned. The barrel lowered, then rose again, then fell to his side. Jordy stepped closer to him.

Typically late, his dad said. And interrupting my work as usual.

He paused, suddenly changing tack. **Come on, son, better late than** never, eh? Stand by me.

Jordy pushed himself upright, eye to eye **with his father. His shoul**ders were drawn back and staunch, but **it was obviously an effort. He** looked over at Alana. She stared back, **silent, poised. Then he gave** Witi a look like he was about to take the **heaviest wave in his life.**

Nah, he said to Witi, before facing his **old man. He shook his head** subtly. Nah, he repeated. Look around you.

His dad smiled, a smile that must've **sealed a billion dollars of** corporate agreements. He beckoned.

Jordan, he said, you and I can share this **moment together. The** moment that everything else has led to. The moment **your mother** first created when she discovered that ancient dimensions **exist. And** with my work we can now control the elements. We're saving **the** world, going to make it better than before. You've got front seats to history. C'mon, you're my boy. My son.

Jordy looked at the soldiers keeping a tight hold on the circle of whānau with their rifles.

Count me out.

Hey, c'mon now. Don't let your mother's death be in vain. She wanted it this way. We were a team. We're this close.

You married her work, not her. You weren't even assed being there when I spread her ashes.

Jordan, I haven't got time for you —

That's an understatement.

At that moment Witi's body convulsed and he took a huge gasp of air. The weirdest warm feeling ever came from deep within his bones to the tip of each strand of hair on his limbs.

Then I'll do it myself, Jordy's dad said, and suddenly the gun was back at Witi's head. I should've done this to start with.

But Jordy's dad stumbled back. Like he was suddenly in shock. Scared. He tripped over Koro's legs and hit the ground, miraculously without pulling the trigger.

You, he cried, up on one elbow and hoisting the pistol.

Jordy crash-tackled Witi to the ground. A big fuckin' hit as the pistol shot exploded around them. Witi thought one or all of the soldiers had hit him – he couldn't breathe – but when Jordy got off him his dad was still aiming up. Like Witi was still up there.

All his family were crouched and cowering. Even some of the soldiers.

But not Witi's dad.

He was there, where Witi had been. Exact same spot, in a magnificent translucent hue. The pistol went off again and Witi saw the ripple of the bullet as it travelled through his dad's forehead and out the back of his head and off into the sky. Jordy's dad tried to let off more rounds but there was only an empty click.

Alana must've sensed the opportunity 'cos she leapt and grabbed the pistol with both hands, stomped a foot on his stomach and yanked the gun from his grasp. She biffed it far down the beach.

What the hell is *that*? Witi **heard Jordy say.**

Witi looked around at everyone.

Wait, you can see my dad? Actual?

Who? Jordy asked.

People were uncovering their heads **and slowly rising**
Someone called out and that's when the **talking and pointing**
Witi's dad was a glowing human shape, **a silhouette with**
much detail as a shop mannequin, but those **in the know knew**
They knew it was his old man.

His mum left Koro and stood silently. She **looked at Witi, like she**
had so many questions but didn't know where to start. **Her eyes be-**
gan to glisten. She turned back to her husband and **they stared at**
each other. Then his mum stepped closer and gently **held a hand to**
his face and he leant his head into the palm. That was when Witi's
mum's waterworks really started.

Witi became aware of others moving around him, and more ghostly
shapes appearing. They moved with purpose, like they had a job to
do. Four of them went to Koro and with two on each side raised him
onto the green surfboard. They lifted it like a stretcher and walked
slowly towards the ocean. Family and soldiers stepped back to form
an aisle. Witi guessed everyone was in shock because no one was
stopping them.

Except his mum. *Where you taking him? Stop!*

But her husband motioned her back, and even though she

could've walked right through that ghost limb she took it no further, but stood and watched with the rest of them.

Except she had to do something:

Whakarongo mai rā te moana kei waho e, she cried as she broke into waiata.

Her grief in every clear word seemed to help the spirits with Koro's weight. Witi's whānau started up as well, joining her in perfect synchronicity like they'd rehearsed it. Over the deep, rousing chanting of the men, his mum's voice rose, clear and staunch. It was beautiful and he desperately wanted to join in.

E āki kau ana ki Te Toka-namu-a-Mihi-marino ...

The few soldiers with their guns still up lowered them in submission. Some must've already fled the scene. Nah, couldn't stand the cultural blast they were getting, eh.

They took Koro out into the foreshore. The water rose to meet the bottom of the board and as they travelled out his ancestors began to dissolve and fade into the water. Even out of sight, Witi could tell they still accompanied Koro, guiding him towards the horizon.

His dad followed them, tailing the last of the group. He never tried to say goodbye. Not even one last wave. Just followed the rest.

His mum fell to her knees at the water's edge. He knelt beside her and held her close. Alana sidled next to her and did the same. They felt the others move behind them and as his dad disappeared into the ocean the full force of a thunderous haka accompanied Koro.

Only when the haka had faded and the men had relaxed did they hear the thumping of two helicopters coming over the bush. They circled around before landing on the sand. Armed Offender cops poured out. Some of the family thought they'd done it themselves, grabbed Jordy's dad, heaved him up off the sand and held him out like an offering. He was escorted onto one of the helicopters and as the engines charged up again and the vessel lifted into the air, Jordy's dad gave his son one last look. Then it was gone and over the hills.

Witi made his way to Jordy, still staring at the sky, standing like the statue he'd promised to become. Witi nudged Jordy's shoulder with his own.

All right?

Mate, and I thought you had issues, he said.

The wail of the engine from the other helicopter grew louder. One of the cops was calling and waving everyone over while another rounded them up and ushered some inside. Last train out of here and Witi wasn't keen on taking one more step up that bloody hill. He made sure his mum was in safely, with family around her. He raised a thumb at her and she gave him a tired smile back.

One last look.

That's all Witi wanted before he climbed into the belly of the helicopter – a final goodbye to the horizon. To Koro. To his dad. He wanted to watch the next black line of a wave enter the bay and to make an agreement with it that neither would see the other again.

Just a rogue wave, by itself. It was rare thing. But this wave …

Yeah, this wave …

its peak was building higher and quicker than the rest. And its
tapered length stretched from one end of the bay to the other. This
wave was gonna be just perfect.

C'mon kidz

And suddenly the cloud broke apart and the last of the day's sunlight danced like fallen stars on its face. They grew in numbers as the
wave rose to the sky.

Witi! Witi, get in!

It was gonna be something special, definitely worth holding a
bird full of people up for.

Witi

Witi

He heard his name in his head, over the roar of the blades above
him. The ocean was calling him again.

Witi

They hadn't finished with him. The souls, maybe the old man. He
broke free of the hand that had reached out to pull him inside, and
ran back to the foreshore.

He watched as the tip of the wave began to fall and pull the rest
of the lip over on itself before running down the line of the wave
like giant fingers pounding up a piano keyboard. Musta formed the
biggest freakin' barrel ever. It was a beautiful sight.

And out of the barrel the silhouette of a surfer appeared in bright sunlight.

Witi squinted. He lunged into the ocean. Anything to get clarity on what he was seeing. Watching as the surfer drew arcs and lines along the face of the wave. Controlling the pace and the fall of the lip, disappearing behind the wave's curtain, only to reappear seemingly at will. Witi could make out the green of the surfboard but this wasn't Koro. He mighta talked himself up and told Witi he once surfed like that back in the day, but he couldn't do it like this. Not now. Not in the state they saw him enter the ocean in. This surfer was making the board dance.

Mum was suddenly beside him in the water, watching as the...

You think ...

Yes, son, she said. Yes! He's coming. He's coming back to us.

'RE NOT THERE

It was the same this dance of his dad wading out of the shorebreak, Witi was sure of it. But this time he could make out dark hair, straight and attached, and the pale skin tone of a bare torso, and muscle definition down the right arm as it cradled the green board. When Witi saw the footprints left behind in the wet sand he knew there was no question, Dad had to be real.

Witi's mum was fidgety-as, like a race horse in a starting gate. She took a step forward and then another. Stopped. One more step. Suddenly she was certain and started running.

Witi was only a few paces behind.

His mum touched his dad's face and Witi saw her fingers run through his beard hair. He musta felt real too. His father's hand reached out and cradled the back of her neck.

He never stopped believing you'd come home, Witi's mum said. And I wished. Every day.

Witi watched him stare back at her, like maybe he was falling into her eyes for the first time again. He eventually looked at Witi and then his gaze fell back over his shoulder towards the horizon.

I'm already home, he said.

No, his mum said, no. You can't be. We're not there.

Not yet you're not.

He held the surfboard out towards Witi. Helluva performance on this. You did good. He gave a faint smile.

Witi took it from him. Coulda used me in the band, huh?

Nah, I shoulda been in yours.

But you're coming back with us, right? Witi asked. Cos you're here now. You're real.

His father put his hand on Witi's shoulder. He pulled him and his mum in and held them.

Not yet, he said. But soon.

He kissed them each on their heads and stepped back.

But why? Witi asked. I don't understand. He motioned to his mum. We don't understand.

Actually, I think I do, son, she said. And she stepped forward and kissed her husband.

This is bullshit, Witi said. He pulled the carving over his head and held it out. Here, he said.

Hold onto it, his father replied. You'll need it.

I don't want it.

But his dad didn't even look at it. You've got much more to know. Others to meet.

When?

Soon, pal. Very soon.

Witi heard a yell from back towards the helicopter. Time had run out and they needed to leave.

Soon, his father promised again and he turned towards the ocean. Witi and his mum watched him enter the water and as each step got deeper they saw strands of sparkled tones of cyan and yellow-white be drawn to him, surrounding him in light until he disappeared into the first wave of the shorebreak.

TAKE THAT SILVER LINING

Koro's tangi was held back on the coast. The only building to survive the storm stood staunch just like he was. Like a totara tree, he woulda said. Through heavy rain, Witi looked back up the beach from where they were all gathered. The whare glowed and waited for them.

There was no body to weep over or to touch or kiss. Nothing physical to farewell. Instead there were flowers and flax weaves pushed into the outgoing tide and lots of waiata and rousing haka — fit for royalty, Witi reckoned. One of the aunties said the rain was the tears from their heaven, giving respect to Koro and his mana, and everyone nodded and agreed with her.

Witi thought of those who'd been there — whānau who'd seen Koro's heroics — explaining to the others what had happened.

Geez, imagine being on the end of that story.

Everyone would've had their own interpretation of it too, whether storyteller or listener. With adults involved there was always going to be a pile of judgement that would bend the reality, confusing the true heroes and the guilty.

But they must've come to their own conclusions because even now, as Witi took stabs of glances from the safety of his hoody, there was always someone staring back at him.

Like he was a fucking con artist. Like all of this was his fault.

His mum must've felt it too. She squeezed him into her so they made a wall of defiance together. She was farewelling her father, but she also had her son back and the hope of a husband one day and no suspicious glare was gonna take that silver lining away from her.

Yeah, from us, Witi thought.

Back in the whare the food trays of seafood, meat and stacks of vegetables sat pretty much untouched on the tables. The fogged-up windows had dried off again and it looked like tomorrow the pigs were gonna be the real winners from this occasion.

Witi stood in the corner by the entrance. He was wary of being trapped if he went further in. His mum hung close by, doing her best bridge impersonation, trying to be civilised and win some of the whānau over. But she'd been away too long. When the arguing started up and the warm talk turned to shouting, Witi was relieved he hadn't been able to convince Alana to be here.

'Nah, it's a time for you to reconnect with your whānau,' she'd said. 'Next time though, hun.'

And he'd been so stoked, 'cos she'd never called him that before, that the urge to try and sway her disappeared. It made him happy just recalling it.

See! Look at him smiling. He thinks it's all a laugh, dontcha !

One of the uncles was up on a chair and pointing at Witi and now everyone was staring his way.

He slid out the door and into the darkness. His mum took the opportunity to slink out too before things turned real nasty.

Witi hadn't got far. His mum found him standing under the roof-line, staring out into the night with its silver dashes of rain still falling. Like the noise inside, the ocean had grown louder, pounding on the shore.

They're still calling me, he said. Dad's there. I can hear him.

You don't have to be afraid anymore, son.

Witi put an arm around her.

And neither do you.

ACKNOWLEDGEMENTS

Before this book found its way into your hands, it first passed across the following people who all played important roles in its journey, and who I am eternally thankful to.

The first people I always have the highest gratitude to are Barbara and Chris Else who have been encouraging mentors for me as a writer and unrelentingly honest and loyal as my agents over many years.

A big shout out goes to my lifelong mate and surfing buddy Nick Kneesch who took the early draft for a paddle and came back with a thumbs up. Next wave's yours, bro.

To Christine Dale and Jenny Nagle from One Tree House — thank you for believing in the story and my vision and for allowing your super talented editing and design team to bring it all to life.

I'm grateful for my parent-in-laws Ian and Helen Perry who assisted me with the cultural themes in the story and who have also, along with our wider whānau, given me an appreciation of Māoritanga over many years.

And most importantly to my wife Jo and our boys Taylor and Toby — you're a constant source of inspiration for me. Love you guys.

Lastly, to all the teachers and librarians who work hard day after day keeping literature relevant to each new generation of student, particularly reluctant readers. They will never forget you and that book.

ABOUT THE AUTHOR AARON TOPP

Aaron is an award-winning author and former teacher who lives in Hawke's Bay where he is a keen surfer.

His first book, *Single Fin* (Random House, 2006), won the New Zealand Post Book Awards for Children and Young Adults YA Fiction Honour Award (2007) , and was also listed as a 2007 Storylines Notable Young Adult Fiction Book. He then released a nonfiction title *Creating Waves: How Surfing Inspires our Most Creative New Zealanders* (HarperCollins, 2009) and in 2015 the mountain biking-themed *Hucking Cody* (Mary Egan Publishing), which received a Storylines Notable Book Award and was a finalist for the New Zealand Book Awards for Children and Young Adults, YA Fiction Award in 2016.